Futa Hunter Mega Anthology

Amanda Strom

Published by Amanda Strom, 2024.

FUTA HUNTER MEGA ANTHOLOGY

First edition. February 20, 2024.

Copyright © 2024 Amanda Strom.

ISBN: 979-8227993427

Written by Amanda Strom.

Table of Contents

Futa Hunter: Shy Teacher

Samantha sauntered into the language school, her piercing blue eyes scanning the room. A dozen students milled about, chatting and flipping through textbooks as they waited for class to begin.

Her gaze settled on the teacher, a shy young woman with soft brown hair and gentle eyes. Melissa. Samantha smiled, warmth pooling between her legs. Her target.

She took a seat in the front row, crossing her legs to give Melissa a tantalizing glimpse of smooth inner thigh. Melissa flushed, looking away as she rearranged papers on her desk.

When class began, Samantha leaned forward, batting her lashes at Melissa. "¿Cómo estás, Señorita?" she purred.

Melissa's cheeks turned scarlet. "B-bien, gracias. Y tú?"

"Excelente." Samantha traced a finger down her neckline. Melissa stammered through roll call, her eyes flicking to Samantha again and again.

As Melissa explained Spanish greetings, Samantha undid another button on her blouse. A swell of arousal rose within as she glimpsed Melissa's nipples hardening beneath her modest blouse.

When Melissa asked if there were any questions, Samantha raised her hand. "¿Qué significa cuando dices que estás 'caliente'?" She arched a brow.

The other students tittered as Melissa sputtered. "E-eso es... un tema inapropiado para la clase."

"Lo siento, Señorita." Samantha grinned. "I'll be sure to ask you after class."

Melissa hurried through the rest of her lesson, stumbling over words as her cheeks burned. The ache between Samantha's legs intensified.

Soon the students were filing out, but Samantha lingered. Melissa busied herself erasing the chalkboard, trembling under Samantha's smoldering gaze.

Samantha slid up beside her, breathing in Melissa's scent. "About my question..."

Melissa fumbled with the eraser. "Please, this is highly inappropriate."

"Is it?" Samantha traced a finger down Melissa's arm. "Oh, you got the wrong idea. I really am interested in Spanish slang. I mean, if we are to use the language in the real world, we need to know how people actually talk, don't we?"

Melissa shivered, color flooding her cheeks. "You are correct, but this is not the focus of today's lesson."

Samantha leaned closer, her lips brushing Melissa's ear. "But I'd love a private lesson. Don't you want to teach me?"

Melissa whimpered. "I shouldn't..."

"Please?" Samantha caressed Melissa's waist, thrilling at the softness beneath her fingers. "I'm such a dedicated student."

Melissa hesitated, then nodded. She stood stiff as a board, clutching her books to her chest. Samantha sidled up to her, pulse racing. She traced a finger down Melissa's cheek. "You're even more beautiful up close."

Melissa gasped, color flooding her cheeks. "W-we should not be doing this."

"Doing what?" Samantha feathered kisses along Melissa's neck, delighting in each soft moan. "I just want to learn."

Melissa's books tumbled to the floor as she gripped Samantha's shoulders. Samantha slid her hands up Melissa's skirt, teasing the sensitive flesh of her inner thighs.

"Please," Melissa whimpered. "We can't—"

Samantha silenced her with a deep, claiming kiss.

Melissa stiffened, panic flashing in her eyes. "I'm sorry, I should not have—you should go—"

"Shh." Samantha nuzzled against her neck. "It's okay. I want this. I want you."

Melissa shook her head, eyes squeezed shut. "No, I can't—there's something wrong with me—"

"There's nothing wrong with you." Samantha grasped Melissa's chin, forcing her to meet her gaze. "You're perfect."

Melissa whimpered. "You don't understand."

"Then show me." Samantha captured Melissa's mouth in a searing kiss, pinning her in place. Melissa struggled half-heartedly, nerves melting into desire, and Samantha deepened the kiss.

A soft moan escaped Melissa's lips. The tension seeped from her body as she surrendered to the passion coursing between them.

Samantha slid her hand between Melissa's legs, teasing her slick folds. Melissa jerked, a strangled cry catching in her throat. Samantha stroked faster, relishing each soft gasp and whimper.

"Please," Melissa moaned. "I can't—it's too much—"

"Shh, I've got you." Samantha quickened her pace, biting down on Melissa's neck. Melissa whimpered, her eyes fluttering shut. Samantha took the opportunity to crash their lips together, swallowing Melissa's moan of surrender.

They stumbled together toward the desk, knocking over stacks of papers in their haste to undress one another. Samantha bent Melissa over the desk, lavishing open-mouthed kisses over her neck and shoulders.

She slid two fingers inside Melissa's wet heat, pumping into her slowly. Melissa cried out, rocking back to meet each thrust. Samantha quickened her pace, curling her fingers to stroke that sensitive spot inside.

Melissa tensed, her inner walls clamping down around Samantha's fingers. But just before climax, she pulled away with a gasp. "I'm sorry, I can't—"

Samantha shushed her gently, stroking her sides. "It's alright, I understand." She pressed a soft kiss to Melissa's shoulder. "Have you ever had an orgasm before?"

Melissa flushed, averting her gaze. She gave a tiny shake of her head.

"There's nothing to be ashamed of." Samantha tilted Melissa's chin up, gazing into her eyes. "Many women have trouble climaxing at first. But I can show you how, if you'll let me."

Melissa swallowed, desire warring with nerves in her expression. "I—there's something you should know. Whenever I get close, I feel something...changing. Inside me." She bit her lip. "It scares me, and that's why I always pull away."

Samantha smiled, a predatory gleam in her eyes. "I know. And there's nothing to fear. What you're feeling is completely natural for a woman like yourself."

"A woman like me?" Melissa echoed faintly.

"You're special, Melissa." Samantha traced a finger down her cheek. "You were born to experience pleasure in a way most women can only dream of. But you have to let go, and embrace what you truly are." Her hand drifted lower, fingers brushing the juncture of Melissa's thighs. "Will you trust me?"

Melissa swallowed hard, gazing up at Samantha through half-lidded eyes. She gave a tiny nod.

"Good girl." Samantha kissed her, slow and deep, and slid two fingers inside her. Melissa gasped into the kiss, rocking forward to meet each thrust. Samantha stroked and curled, building the pressure inside her.

Melissa tensed as the now-familiar feeling rose within her, but Samantha pressed closer, pinning her in place. "Don't fight it," she breathed against Melissa's lips. "Let go."

Melissa whimpered, trembling on the edge of climax. Her body burned, consumed by need, but still she resisted, afraid of the unknown that awaited her.

Samantha nipped at her jaw, fingers pumping relentlessly. "Come for me, Melissa. Embrace what you are and come for me." Her voice was rough with desire, brooking no refusal.

Melissa squeezed her eyes shut, caught between ecstasy and terror. But Samantha's touch left her no choice. Pleasure crested and broke over her in a devastating wave, shattering her resistance.

As her inner walls spasmed around Samantha's fingers, something emerged from within her, sliding out in a gush of wetness. She cried out at the strangeness of it, eyes flying open—and saw, to her shock, a thick cock jutting from between her legs.

Samantha purred in satisfaction, wrapping her hand around Melissa's new appendage and stroking firmly. "There, now. Isn't that better?"

Melissa could only stare, stunned into silence. She felt the weight of it, the sensitivity, as if she'd had it all her life. Yet her mind reeled at the impossibility.

"You're a futa, darling," Samantha crooned, "A woman gifted with the best of both worlds. And now that you've awakened, there's no limit to the pleasure you can experience." She squeezed the base of Melissa's cock, wringing a choked moan from her throat. "You were made for this."

Melissa swallowed hard, struggling to find her voice. "But how...how is this possible?"

Samantha's lips curled into a feline smile. "No one knows for sure. Some believe they born this way, others that it's a mutation. All that matters is that futas are superior lovers, uniquely equipped to bring their partners the ultimate in carnal delight. And you will pay me back for awakening you."

Her fingers danced up Melissa's length again, lighting sparks of pleasure behind her eyes. "My dear, have a gorgeous cock. So big and thick and aching to be used." Samantha shifted to straddle Melissa's lap, the heat of her sex searing Melissa's sensitive flesh. "I think it's time you learned how pleasurable it can be to bury yourself in a warm, willing cunt."

Melissa's breath caught at the vulgarity, cheeks flushing pink. She tried to protest, but coherent thought deserted her as Samantha rocked against her, slick folds caressing her cock.

"Don't be afraid to take what you need." Samantha's lips brushed the shell of her ear, voice dropping to a sultry purr. "In fact, I demand it. Fuck me now."

The order sent a bolt of heat straight to Melissa's cock. She growled low in her throat, hands flying to Samantha's hips, and slammed up into her without thinking.

Samantha cried out in ecstasy, inner walls flexing around Melissa's length. "Yes, that's it! Fuck me, darling, fuck me as hard as you can!"

Spurred on by Samantha's cries, Melissa drove up into her again and again, utterly lost to the delicious friction and tight heat enveloping her cock. She hissed through her teeth at the intensity of it, chasing her own pleasure as much as her mentor's.

Samantha clutched at her shoulders, meeting each brutal thrust with equal fervor. "So perfect," she panted, eyes glazed with lust. "You were born to do this, to fuck and be fucked. A futa's purpose is pleasure, and you fulfill it so beautifully!"

As they fucked, Melissa couldn't help but revel in the sensation of being both the one taking and giving pleasure. Her mind was a jumble of emotions, trying to make sense of the newfound knowledge about herself, but her body knew only ecstasy. She moaned Samantha's name, her eyes rolling back in her head as she felt the intense pleasure coursing through her system. The friction between their bodies was exquisite, the slapping sounds echoing in the empty classroom filling her ears.

Samantha's fingers dug into her shoulders, urging her on, and Melissa obliged, slamming into her harder. Their sweat-slick skin smelled intoxicating, a heady mixture of arousal and fear and anticipation. Her hips bucked up to meet each powerful thrust, feeling herself getting closer to the edge again.

"Yes!" Samantha cried out as Melissa's cock rubbed against her g-spot with every thrust, sending waves of pleasure coursing through her. "Fuck yes!"

Melissa couldn't believe how natural it felt to fuck a woman with her big cock. She never had to move her hips like that before, but now she felt like a relentless fucking machine, striving to pound faster and harder.

Samantha groaned, her feet digging into the floor as Melissa's cock pistoned in and out of her, pounding her pussy with a ferocity that sent waves of pleasure coursing through her body. Her own hips snapped back to meet each powerful thrust, her breath catching in her throat as the sensation grew more and more intense. She could feel the heat radiating from Melissa's body, the slick sounds filling the empty classroom echoing in her ears.

"More," she gasped, pushing herself up on tiptoes so that Melissa's cock could get even deeper. "That's it, darling. Give it to me."

Melissa grunted, her eyes squeezed shut as she lost herself in the motion. She could feel Samantha's walls clamping down on her cock with each stroke, sending electric shocks through every nerve ending inside of her. Her own cunt was on fire now, hot and wet and aching for release. The sound of skin slapping against skin filled the room, muffled only by their frantic gasps for air.

Melissa was lost in the rhythm now, mindless with lust and need. Every time their bodies collided, sending shockwaves of pleasure rippling across their skin, she wanted to scream with delight. It felt so good to take control like this; to be dominant instead of submissive for once. A thrill ran through her at the idea of pleasuring another woman like this - a woman like Samantha who seemed to crave it just as much as she did.

Samantha's breath hitched as Melissa's thrusts became more desperate, driving her toward the precipice of orgasm. She raked her nails down Melissa's back, leaving red welts in their wake, a testament to the passion that consumed them. But Samantha wanted more—needed more.

"Harder!" Samantha gasped, arching her back to meet Melissa's powerful thrusts. "I want to feel you deep inside me. Give it to me, Melissa!"

Melissa growled in response, her movements becoming primal and urgent. She gripped Samantha's hips possessively, guiding her with an unyielding force that bordered on dominance.

The tension coiled within Melissa grew unbearable, a white-hot fire building at the base of her spine. She could feel her release building, the pressure mounting with each thrust. Samantha's body quivered beneath her, her moans growing louder and more desperate.

With one final, powerful thrust, Melissa felt the dam break.Pleasure surged through her veins, consuming her from head to toe. She cried out in ecstasy as her orgasm washed over her, pulsing through her cock and spilling into Samantha's waiting depths. It was her first orgasm with a cock and it made her explode with a force of a thousand suns. Melissa's entire body was on fire, each nerve ending tingling and alive. The pleasure was like a supernova, a bursting star of ecstasy that radiated through her body and lit up the entire universe. It was a primal and all-encompassing ecstasy, a force so powerful and all-consuming that it left her gasping for air and trembling with the intensity of it all. In that moment, she knew that this was what true ecstasy felt like, and she never wanted it to end.

Samantha's body tensed beneath her, a symphony of pleasure and release echoing through the room as she found her own climax. Her walls contracted around Melissa's cock, milking every last drop of pleasure from their union.

As their bodies slowly stilled, Melissa collapsed onto Samantha, their sweat-slicked skin sticking together. A sense of euphoria washed over her, mingling with the realization of what had just transpired.

Samantha grinned and pushed Melissa to the side. "What are you doing? I didn't tell you to stop fucking?"

"But I just came!"

"So what? You are a futa, not a man! Look, your cock is still ready."

Melissa looked down and indeed, her enormous and cum-drenched cock was as hard as before. Melissa's eyes widened at the sight of her still throbbing cock. Samantha was right. She wasn't like men. The post-orgasmic haze began to clear, replaced by a renewed hunger for pleasure coursing through her veins.

Samantha smirked, her eyes filled with mischief. "Don't keep me waiting, Melissa. I want to feel you inside me again."

Without another word, Samantha positioned herself on all fours, presenting her luscious curves and dripping cunt to Melissa. The sight alone was enough to make her cock twitch with anticipation. She moved behind Samantha, running her hands along the smooth skin of her rounded ass.

Melissa growled softly as she pressed her tip against Samantha's entrance, relishing the tight heat that awaited her. She leaned forward and pressed a lingering kiss to Samantha's neck, ears, and shoulders, enjoying the taste of her skin mixed with sweat and desire. Then she slowly pushed inside, feeling the warmth and wetness engulf her cock as it slid into Samantha's pussy, still filled with Melissa's warm cum. Samantha moaned, arching her back and pushing back against her.

With a groan, Melissa started moving, finding a rhythm that felt natural and powerful. Her hips snapped back and forth, driving herself deeper into Samantha's welcoming heat with every thrust. She could feel every inch of her cock sinking into the woman who'd shown her this new world of pleasure. Melissa leaned down and bit at Samantha's shoulder, their skin tearing slightly as she claimed her mentor as her own.

Melissa slammed into Samantha over and over, her hips snapping back to meet each powerful thrust. She felt her cock rub against Samantha's g-spot, sending waves of pleasure coursing through her body. The friction between their skin was electric, igniting every nerve ending with each slap and smack. Their sweat mingled on their skin, a heady mixture of arousal and need. The scent of sex filled the air as they fucked like animals in heat, their gasps for air only punctuating the rhythm they had found. Melissa planted kisses along Samantha's spine, nipping playfully at her flesh as she moved faster. Her hips bucked up to meet each powerful thrust, loving the feel of being both dominant and submissive at once.

"Yes!" Samantha cried out, arching her back to meet every thrust. "Fuck me harder!"

The tension inside Melissa grew unbearable once again, a white-hot fire building at the base of her spine. She could feel herself getting close to climax again as she pounded into Samantha's pussy. With one final thrust, she released another powerful orgasm that coursed through her body like lightning striking twice in one night. It left her trembling and panting for breath, every nerve ending tingling with pleasure. This time she didn't stop though.

She kept fucking as cock pushed her seed out of Samantha's cunt with each thrust.

Melissa's thrusts became even more relentless as she was overcome with the insatiable hunger for pleasure. Samantha's moans grew louder, her body trembling beneath Melissa's powerful onslaught. She reveled in the sensation of being taken so forcefully, allowing herself to surrender completely to the overwhelming pleasure that consumed her.

This is why she did what she did, why she hunted innocent, uninitiated futas and unleashed them.

Only a fresh futa could fuck like that.

Melissa's newborn dominant nature took hold once again as she pulled Samantha's hair back, exposing her neck and arching her back further. Her thrusts intensified, fueled by an uncontrollable need to claim and possess her. Melissa watched in awe as Samantha's body writhed beneath her, completely surrendered to the pleasure that pulsed through her veins.

The classroom seemed to fade away, nothing existing but the intense connection between Melissa and Samantha. Despite Melissa's life changing completely, all the question didn't worry her at this moment, because right now she existed only to fuck.

Samantha's eyes widened, her mouth forming an O of pleasure as she was pushed closer to the edge. The intensity of the sensations coursing through her body was overwhelming, pushing her towards a climax that promised to be more earth-shattering than any she had ever experienced before.

With every ounce of strength, Melissa fucked Samantha senseless. She leaned into the kisses she placed on Samantha's shoulder blades and back, her nails digging in slightly, gripping her tightly. There was a primal desire in her eyes as she moved faster and harder, loving the way Samantha's body responded to her touch. Her hips pounded furiously, her cock pistoning in and out of Samantha's warmth, stretching her tightness as it filled with another onslaught of pleasure.

And then Samantha came undone again.

Her body convulsed with the force of her orgasm, a wave of pleasure crashing through her. Her walls clamped down on Melissa's cock in a vice-like grip, milking her for every drop of ecstasy she had to offer.

Melissa continued her powerful thrusts, drawing out Samantha's orgasm as long as she could, reveling in the way her body trembled and shuddered beneath her. Waves of pleasure radiated through Melissa, fueling her own desire to reach new heights of sexual bliss.

As Samantha's climax subsided, Melissa pulled out slowly, savoring the slick sensation of their combined juices dripping from her cock.

"Suck me now!" She growled. "Lick me clean, I want to see your lips on my shaft!"

Samantha grinned. No more than fifteen minutes ago this shy Spanish teacher felt embarrassed because a student called her 'hot' in Spanish.

Now, she was a full-fledged futa and this is why Samantha did what she did.

Samantha opened her mouth and wrapped her lips around Melissa's juicy cock.

Melissa watched in fascination as Samantha's lips closed around her cock, slowly taking her in. She bit her bottom lip, looking down at the head of her shaft disappearing into Samantha's eager mouth. Her breath hitched, feeling every stroke of Samantha's tongue on her sensitive skin.

Samantha bobbed her head back and forth, taking Melissa deeper and deeper into her mouth. Her tongue swirled around the sensitive underside of Melissa's cock, sending shivers of pleasure racing up her spine. The thought that she is the first woman ever to suck this magnificent cock drove her insane.

The sound of slurping filled the room as Samantha lapped at every drop of their combined juices from Melissa's engorged cock. Her soft tongue rubbed against the swollen head, making Melissa let out a moan that vibrated throughout Samantha's mouth.

Samantha looked up at Melissa through hooded lids, a gleam of hunger in her eyes that made Melissa's heart race. With one hand, she gently stroked the back of Samantha's head while she held onto the desk for balance.

Suddenly, Samantha's fingers found their way to Melissa's cunt and her world exploded. She was so focused on her new cock that she totally forgot that her pussy is still there, moist and craving attention. Samantha fingered her in rhythm with her sucking, exploring every inch of her slick folds with skillful precision. Melissa's moans grew louder, the pleasure building inside her like an inferno ready to consume her whole.

The dual pleasure overwhelmed her senses, causing her to lose herself in the moment.

Melissa's grip tightened on the edge of the desk as Samantha's fingers plunged deeper into her dripping pussy.

The taste of Melissa's desire mixed with their combined juices was intoxicating to Samantha. She relished in the power she held over Melissa, knowing that she could bring her to the brink of ecstasy and beyond. Her fingers plunged deeper, curling just right to hit that sweet spot inside Melissa that made her gasp and writhe beneath Samantha's touch.

With a final flick of her tongue, Samantha released Melissa's cock from her mouth and pulled away. "It looks clean enough to me. Now, I want to ride you. You are my trophy after all, Melissa. ¿Entiendes?"

Melissa's chest heaved as she caught her breath, her body still buzzing with the remnants of pleasure. She nodded, a smirk playing on her lips. "¡Sí, entiendo perfectamente!" she replied.

Without hesitation, Melissa sat back on the edge of the desk, her legs spread wide, an invitation for Samantha to claim her prize. Samantha wasted no time straddling Melissa's hips, aligning herself with Melissa's wetness. The anticipation hung heavy in the air as she slowly lowered herself, the head of Melissa's cock teasingly brushing against her wet folds. With a moan that mingled with Melissa's eager whimper, Samantha sank down, impaling herself on the throbbing length.

A guttural moan escaped Melissa's lips as she felt Samantha's warm depths envelop her, inch by inch. The sensation was pure bliss, the feeling of being completely consumed by Samantha's tightness overwhelming her senses. The power dynamic between them shifted once again as Samantha took control, rising and falling on Melissa's cock with purposeful grace.

"So, how do you like to be a futa, Melissa?"

Melissa's eyes glazed over with pleasure and a mischievous smile formed on her lips as she locked eyes with Samantha. "Fuck," Melissa managed to breathe out. "This...this is beyond anything I ever imagined. I can't wait to fuck all the cunts I can get."

Samantha leaned forward, her hands gripping Melissa's shoulders for support as she continued to ride her cock. Her hips moved in a steady rhythm, grinding against Melissa's pelvis with each delicious thrust. "Mmm, that's what I wanted to hear," she whispered, her warm breath fanning across Melissa's ear.

Melissa's hands traveled up Samantha's sides, tracing the curve of her waist before gripping the softness of her breasts. She kneaded them gently, reveling in the hardness of Samantha's nipples.

Their bodies moved in perfect synchrony, a dance of pleasure and desire. Samantha's moans filled the room, mixing with Melissa's grunts of satisfaction. Melissa's grip tightened on Samantha's breasts, her nails digging into the supple flesh. She reveled in the way Samantha arched her back, offering herself completely to the pleasure they were creating together. The heat between them was electric, crackling with a raw energy that fueled their lustful desires.

Samantha's head fell back, her long hair cascading down her back as she surrendered herself to Melissa's touch. Her walls clenched around Melissa's cock, pulsing with an urgency that matched the fire in their bodies.

Samantha claimed her prize, a newborn futa, another notch on her belt.

She moved faster and faster, knowing that the orgasm to come will be the strongest of them all.

Their bodies collided in perfect harmony, Samantha's hips pistoning up and down on Melissa's throbbing cock. The desk creaked under their fervent movements as they sought release.

Samantha leaned forward, her breasts brushing against Melissa's chest with each thrust. Her nipples were hardened buds against Melissa's palms, straining for attention but not getting enough. Melissa wanted to suckle them, bite them, use them to her advantage as Samantha rode her. Melissa felt Samantha's cunt grip her like a vice. She could feel herself getting close to the edge again but wanted this moment to last forever.

Samantha's pace quickened, her body tensing as she chased her release. Melissa could feel the urgency in her movements, the desperation to reach that pinnacle of ecstasy. With a final, forceful thrust, Samantha let out a cry of pure bliss as her orgasm washed over her. With a primal growl, Samantha dug her nails into Melissa's shoulders, arching her back as waves of pleasure crashed over her. Her inner muscles contracted around Melissa's cock, milking her for all she was worth once again.

The sight of Samantha unraveling on top of her was all it took for Melissa to tip over the edge. Her grip tightened on Samantha's hips as she felt her own climax crashing through her. Wave after wave of pleasure surged through her, consuming her completely.

As their bodies trembled in the aftermath, they clung to each other, sweat-slicked, cum-slicked and breathless.

"Okay Melissa, I know you want more, but I'm done for today. I need to rest, and you have a lot to process. Though I bet you'll spend the night playing with your new toy instead."

Melissa grinned. "What are you doing tomorrow?"

"Meeting with my new landlord."

The End.

Futa Hunter: Feisty Landlord

Samantha smirked as she hauled another box up the steps to her new apartment. This was the place. She could feel it.

Ava stood at the top of the stairs, arms crossed, foot tapping impatiently. "Hurry up! I don't have all day."

"My apologies, Ms. Martinez." Samantha put on her most charming smile and brushed past Ava to enter the apartment. Ava's scent enveloped her—sandalwood and jasmine. Intoxicating with a hint of an uninitiated futa.

As Samantha unpacked her books, Ava prowled around the apartment, inspecting for any damage. Samantha stretched, exposing a strip of toned midriff. Ava's gaze snapped to the flash of skin before she looked away, cheeks coloring.

Interesting.

"The rent is due on the first of the month," Ava snapped. "No pets, no noise, no—"

"Parties, I know." Samantha sauntered over until she stood just behind Ava, close enough to feel the warmth radiating from her body. She lowered her voice to a husky whisper. "Don't worry, Ms. Martinez. I'll be on my best behavior."

Ava whirled around, eyes flashing. "Look, I don't know what kind of game you're playing, but I won't tolerate any funny business. If you cause me trouble, you'll be out on your ear."

Samantha merely smiled. Ava was fighting it, but the attraction was there. Her true futa nature was awakening.

It was only a matter of time.

Ava threw up her hands. "Just get your things unpacked! I have better things to do than stand here all day." She stormed out, slamming the door behind her.

Samantha chuckled. The game was afoot. This was going to be fun.

The next day, Samantha "accidentally" broke the pipes under the kitchen sink, flooding the apartment. She turned off the water and called Ava, feigning distress.

Ava arrived in a fury, eyes blazing as she took in the mess. "What did you do?" She shrieked.

Samantha blinked guileless blue eyes. "I'm so sorry, Ms. Martinez. I was trying to fix the leak, and the pipe just burst. I'll pay for the damages, of course."

"Like hell you will!" Ava grabbed Samantha's arm, and a jolt of electricity shot between them. Ava's fingers tightened before she wrenched her hand away.

"There's no need to get violent," Samantha purred. She moved closer, watching Ava's chest rise and fall with harsh breaths. "I just want to make things right."

Ava's eyes narrowed. "The only way to make this right is to leave. Now."

Samantha tsked. "Come now, that's no way to solve problems. You're all worked up. Why don't you let me give you a massage? It will help you relax."

"A massage?" Ava sputtered. "I don't think so."

"I'm very good with my hands." Samantha reached out and ran a finger down Ava's arm. Ava shivered, eyes darkening with desire. "Just say yes."

Ava hesitated, suspicion warring with arousal on her face. Finally, she gritted out a single word: "Fine."

Samantha smiled, a surge of victory flooding her veins. The futa beast within Ava was awakening at last.

"Excellent choice," she purred, guiding Ava toward the bedroom. The game had only just begun.

Samantha closed the bedroom door behind them with a soft click. Ava stood awkwardly in the middle of the room, arms crossed over her chest, glare fixed on Samantha.

"No need to be shy," Samantha said. She slid her hands up Ava's arms, feeling the tension in her muscles. Ava tensed but didn't pull away. "Just relax and enjoy."

Samantha slowly undressed Ava, peeling away her shirt and bra to reveal full, supple breasts. She cupped them in her hands, kneading and squeezing until Ava's nipples hardened under her touch.

A gasp escaped Ava's lips. She arched into the sensation, eyes fluttering shut. Samantha smiled, trailing one hand down Ava's torso to slide under the waistband of her pants.

"You're so wet already," Samantha purred, fingers gliding through Ava's slick folds. Ava moaned, spreading her legs to give Samantha better access.

"This was your plan all along, wasn't it?" Ava said breathlessly. Her hips rocked against Samantha's hand, urging her deeper.

"Guilty as charged." Samantha slid two fingers inside Ava's entrance, pumping slowly. Ava cried out, gripping Samantha's shoulders to stay upright.

"I knew...there was something about you," Ava gasped out between thrusts. Her inner walls clenched around Samantha's fingers, drawing them in greedily.

Samantha increased her pace, curling her fingers to stroke Ava's sweet spot. Ava shuddered violently, hips bucking as ecstasy flooded her body.

Her moans filled the room, growing louder with each stroke of Samantha's skilled fingers. Ava clung to Samantha, her body trembling with pleasure as Samantha kissed the side of Ava's neck.

Samantha could feel the pulse racing through Ava's veins, the heat radiating from her skin. She leaned closer, her lips brushing against Ava's earlobe. "You're mine now," she whispered, her voice thick with possessiveness.

Ava's breathing grew more ragged, her grip on Samantha's shoulders tightening. Samantha could sense that Ava was on the brink of a powerful release. Her own desire surged, matching Ava's intensity.

She knew that she is about to claim her prize, but she still needed to land a killing blow, and so she began fingering Ava with renewed intensity.

Samantha grinned wickedly, her touches becoming more insistent as she felt Ava's body tremble and shudder under her ministrations. She increased the pace, relentlessly stroking and massaging Ava's throbbing clit, feeling it grow swollen under her fingers. Meanwhile, she used the other hand to squeeze one of Ava's nipples between her finger and thumb, rolling it gently as she teased the hard bud. The landlord was succumbing to her touch with each passing moment, her cries and gasps filling the room.

"That's it, Ms. Martinez," Samantha purred in her ear. "Let go...let me take care of you."

Just before climax, Ava pushed Samantha away. "Stop, please..."

Samantha grabbed Ava's wrists, pinning them above her head. "Don't fight it," she whispered, maintaining the motion of her hand.

Ava struggled in vain against Samantha's grip. "No, you don't understand. There's something...inside me. I can feel it growing..." Her protests dissolved into a needy moan as Samantha thrust into her again.

"I know," Samantha said soothingly. "You've felt it your whole life, haven't you? The emptiness, the frustration. An ache you couldn't satisfy no matter how hard you tried. You like sex, you want to submit to desire, but you've never had an orgasm and that's why you are so fucking angry all the fucking time." She leaned in, her lips brushing Ava's ear. "Let go. I'm here to set you free."

Ava went rigid in Samantha's arms, back arching in ecstasy. A muffled scream escaped her as she came undone around Samantha's fingers, inner walls clenching and releasing in powerful spasms.

In the wake of her climax, a bulge formed under Ava's panties. Samantha looked on with lust and satisfaction and as the waves of pleasure receded, Ava became aware of a new sensation between her legs. Something long, thick and heavy lay against her thigh, pulsing in time with her racing heartbeat.

She looked down in disbelief. A massive cock had emerged from her body, fully erect and throbbing, a new and unfamiliar part of her body that felt so right. Then she looked up at Samantha with eyes dark with desire.

"W-what is this?" Ava stammered, staring at the appendage in shock and awe. She gave an involuntary thrust of her hips, the friction against her inner thigh sending a jolt of excitement through her length.

Samantha smiled, eyes gleaming with triumph. "Congratulations, Ms. Martinez. You're no longer just an angry, frustrated woman. You're a futa now." She wrapped her hand around Ava's new cock, giving it an experimental stroke.

Ava cried out at the intense stimulation, bucking into Samantha's grip. It was too much, the pleasure overwhelming after a lifetime of denial.

"There, there," Samantha soothed, tightening her hold. "I know it's a lot to take in, but don't worry. I'm an expert in all things futa. I'll teach you everything you need to know about your new body and abilities." She leaned close, breath hot against Ava's cheek. "But first, I think it's time you paid for your awakening."

Ava frowned in confusion. "Paid? What are you talking about?"

Samantha released Ava's wrists in favor of caressing her cock. "I hunt futas like yourself and awaken them to their true nature. But my services don't come free." Samantha pulled off her blouse, exposing her luscious breasts and hardened nipples. She stepped back, unzipping her skirt and letting it fall to the floor. Samantha was now standing before Ava in nothing but a pair of black lace panties, her desire evident.

Ava's eyes widened as she took in the sight of Samantha's naked body. Her gaze traveled the length of Samantha's smooth skin, lingering on the curve of her hips and the swell of her breasts. The sight sent a surge of desire through her new cock, and she couldn't help but let out a low growl.

Samantha removed her panties and slid onto Ava's lap, positioning her entrance over the swollen head of Ava's cock. "Now, you're going to fuck me with this big dick of yours. Consider it payment for setting you free."

Without waiting for a response, Samantha sank down onto Ava's length in one smooth motion. Ava cried out at the tight heat enveloping her cock, instinct taking over as she began to thrust up into the futa hunter astride her lap.

Samantha moaned, rolling her hips to meet each stroke. "Yes, just like that. Take your pleasure from me, as is your right now." She grasped Ava's face, forcing their gazes to meet. "Welcome to your new life as a futa."

Samantha moaned at the sensation of Ava's cock sliding in and out of her wet pussy, her body meeting each thrust with equal force. The smell of their bodies mingled as they moved together, musk and sweat filling the air. Their skin slapped and stuck together as they fucked, creating a wet sound followed by the rhythmic slapping of flesh against flesh. Samantha's nails dug into Ava's back as she rode her hard, Ava's hips bucking up to meet every stroke.

Her breasts bounced gently with each movement, taunting Samantha who couldn't wait to taste them. She reached down to cup one of them, pinching the nipple gently between her fingers. "That's it, Ava," she urged, taking her own pleasure from the experience. "Now you know what you were missing."

Ava's breathing was ragged as she pounded into Samantha's tight heat, her eyes rolled back in her head in bliss. Her throbbing cock pushed deeper with every thrust, hitting Samantha's cervix with each impact. She growled low in her throat as she felt power surging through her body with each stroke. She had never felt such raw desire before and it was exhilarating.

Samantha wrapped a hand around Ava's base, guiding her hips as she continued to ride her like this was an animalistic display of lust. The landlord groaned against Samantha's lips as they crashed together in a fervent kiss that left both women breathless. Their tongues tangled in a dance of dominance and submission that only fed their passion.

As Ava's cock continued to thrust into Samantha, their kiss deepened, tongues dancing wildly. Their bodies slapped together with wet, slick sounds filling the air. Ava's sharp nails dug into Samantha's back, marking her skin with tiny cuts that only added to the intensity of the encounter.

Samantha moaned against Ava's mouth, feeling the landlord's thick member stretching her walls and filling her completely. She thrust back, meeting every stroke eagerly, grinding her hips against Ava to heighten the sensation. Their chests slapped together in a rhythmic beat that echoed in the small bedroom.

Finally, Samantha broke the kiss and gasped for breath. "That's it, Ava," she panted. "Show me what you're made of." Her eyes traveled down to watch as Ava's huge cock pistoned into her, disappearing inside her again and again in quick powerful thrusts.

She grasped Ava's face once more, holding her gaze as she spoke. "You are mine now," she growled. "Your body obeys my commands." She sat up straight suddenly, looping one of Ava's arms around her neck and pulling back just enough so that only the tip of Ava's cock was still inside her. Then she leaned forward again until their breasts collided, rubbing against each other before slamming back down on Ava's cock with a loud moan.

Ava cried out in response, unable to control herself anymore as Samantha took control of their movements. Samantha's body quivered with anticipation as she rode Ava harder and faster. Her walls clenched around Ava's cock, milking it for every drop of ecstasy she could extract. The heat between them intensified as their bodies moved in perfect harmony, building toward an explosive climax.

Ava couldn't believe the power surging through her body as she felt Samantha's pussy clamp down on her cock, milking her freshly emerged member. She was hungry for more, greedy and desperate as she thrust up to meet Samantha's movements, driving deeper still. Their skin slapped together in quick wet smacks, their bodies moving in perfect synchronicity. Every time Ava's cock slid out of Samantha's pussy, it left a wet trail of desire between them.

Samantha abused Ava's new cock with gusto, riding up and down his shaft with wild abandonment. She cried out in delight with each stroke, her eyes rolling back into her head as she dug deep into Ava's curves.

"Fuck, I'm going to come!"

Just as the words left Samantha's lips, a wave of pleasure crashed over Ava. She could feel the pressure building within her, a powerful surge of electricity coiling in her core. Her muscles tightened, and she gripped Samantha's hips, guiding her movements as she thrust upward with an urgency she had never known.

With each primal thrust, the sensations intensified, ripping through Ava's body like wildfire.

Samantha's eyes widened as she felt Ava's cock pulsate within her, throbbing against her sensitive walls. "Yes! Give it to me!" she cried out, her voice dripping with need. "I want to feel you explode inside me!"

Ava couldn't hold back any longer. Every sensation was heightened, every nerve ending electrified by the pleasure coursing through her veins. With one final thrust, she buried herself deep within Samantha and released herself, her first futa orgasm evaporating her mind into a haze of bliss. Waves of pleasure rolled over her, causing her body to tremble and spasm uncontrollably. Samantha clung to her, moaning in ecstasy as she felt Ava's hot seed fill her, painting her insides with each pulsating spurt.

As their bodies continued to convulse in the aftermath of their release, Ava's mind gradually returned from its euphoric fog. She gazed at Samantha with a mix of awe and gratitude. "I... I don't know what to say," she managed to stutter out, her voice still breathless.

Samantha's eyes sparkled with a mixture of satisfaction and tenderness. She leaned in, capturing Ava's lips in a gentle kiss. "You don't need to say anything," she whispered against Ava's lips. "You need to keep fucking."

"What?"

"Your cock is still hard. Forget anything you know about men, you are a futa, you are a beast, you are made for this."

Ava's mind spun, trying to process the overwhelming sensations and the words that Samantha had just spoken. She had always considered herself a woman, never imagining that she would find herself in this position, with a cock of her own and a hunger she couldn't deny.

Samantha disentangled herself from Ava's embrace, her fingers trailing lightly over Ava's glistening skin. "You have so much power within you," she murmured, her voice husky with desire. "Embrace it, Ava."

Ava's mind was a whirlwind of confusion and desire, but one thing was certain - she couldn't deny how good it felt to be inside Samantha. And so she pushed Samantha on the bed, her eyes enjoying every inch of Samantha's exposed flesh as she laid on her back.

The sight of Samantha spread out before her, her body flushed and glistening with sweat, ignited an insatiable hunger within Ava. She gripped Samantha's thighs, spreading them wider as she leaned in, her lips hovering just above Samantha's wet entrance.

"Please," Samantha begged, her voice desperate and filled with need. "Don't make me wait any longer."

Without hesitation, Ava thrust forward, sinking deep into the sweet cocktail of her own cum and Samantha's wetness that filled her cunt. A low moan escaped Samantha's lips, her body arching against the pleasure coursing through her. Ava reveled in the delicious feeling of being inside her, the walls of Samantha's pussy gripping her cock tightly.

Their bodies moved together with a mix of urgency and reverence, their hips finding a rhythm that left them both gasping for breath. Ava seized control of their movements, setting a relentless pace that pushed them both to the edge of ecstasy. Her hands roamed over Samantha's curves, tracing every contour with a desperate hunger.

Samantha lived for this. To be the first one to touch a new futa's cock, to be the first one fucked by it, to be the first one to gift them their first orgasms.

Samantha was a futa hunter and she would never stop.

Ava was amazed at how natural it felt to fuck a woman. The sensation in her cock, the instinctual movement of her hips, she was a natural.

Time seemed to stand still as they lost themselves in the raw intensity of their union. Each thrust pushed them closer to the edge, building a crescendo of desire that threatened to consume them both. Samantha's fingers dug into Ava's back, leaving trails of fire in their wake. Her nails grazed along Ava's spine, setting off sparks of pleasure that traveled straight to her core.

"Yes, Ava," Samantha gasped, her voice heavy with need. "Faster... harder..."

Ava obliged, quickening the pace of her thrusts. The bed creaked beneath them, matching the rhythm of their bodies as they moved together as one.

Samantha moaned as Ava's cock pistoned in and out of her. The sensation was unlike anything she'd ever felt before, but it was exhilarating. Her breasts bounced with each powerful stroke, leaving a wet trail on Ava's chest as they slapped together.

Ava's hips bucked up to meet Samantha's thrusts, driving herself deeper into the futa hunter. She couldn't believe how good this felt, how right it was. She wanted more and more, her mind lost to the pleasure that consumed her. With a roar, she arched her back and pushed into Samantha harder, claiming her body as hers.

Samantha met every move with equal fervor, their combined moans filling the room. Her teeth sank into her bottom lip, holding back a scream as she felt Ava's cock throbbing inside her. The taste of herself on Ava's tongue only added to the intensity of their connection.

Their pace quickened until they both reached their climaxes at once. Ava's eyes rolled back in her head as she felt herself explode once more, filling Samantha with hot cum again as she cried out in ecstasy. Samantha arched her back off the bed, her own orgasm taking hold of her body like a storm ripping through a city street.

But this time Ava didn't stop, fucking both of them through this monumental orgasm.

Their bodies trembled with the intensity of their simultaneous release, but Ava's hunger was insatiable. She continued to thrust deep into Samantha, riding the waves of pleasure that crashed over them both. Her mind was a blur of sensation, her body riding the wave of ecstasy that crashed over her. The power she felt as a futa coursed through her veins, fueling her insatiable hunger for more. She could hardly believe the depths of pleasure she was capable of inflicting and receiving.

Samantha's eyes fluttered open, a mixture of surprise and awe in her gaze. "You're...still going?" she gasped, her voice laced with pleasure.

Ava grinned. "I had a good teacher. Now turn around, I want to fuck you from behind."

Samantha's breath hitched at Ava's commanding tone. Without a moment's hesitation, she shifted onto her hands and knees, presenting herself to Ava. Her heart raced as she felt the heat of Ava's gaze on her exposed ass, knowing that she was about to be taken in a way that would push her to new heights of pleasure.

Ava positioned herself behind Samantha, guiding her throbbing cock to the entrance of Samantha's cunt. She teased the swollen head along Samantha's folds, relishing in the moans and whimpers that escaped Samantha's lips.

"Please, Ava," Samantha pleaded, her voice strained with need. "Pay me in full. Fuck me."

Ava didn't waste another second. With a swift thrust, she buried herself deep inside Samantha, eliciting a guttural cry from both of them. The sensation of being enveloped by Samantha's tightness was overwhelming.

Samantha moaned loudly as she felt Ava's cock plunge into her from behind. Her pussy clenched around the thick shaft, soaking up every inch of the landlord's pleasure stick. The hot flesh sliding into her felt so right. She braced herself on her hands, pushing back against Ava's thrusts while arching her back to meet her movements. With each stroke, she could feel the heat from Ava's body pulsing in time with her heartbeat.

Ava's hands roamed Samantha's body, tracing curves and pinching nipples as she fucked the futa hunter from behind. The headboard banged against the wall in time with their passionate rhythm. Samantha tossed her head back with each thrust, letting out hoarse cries of pleasure that filled the air around them. She looked over her shoulder at Ava, watching as the landlord pounded into her with wild abandon.

"You feel so fucking good inside of me, Ms. Martinez."

Ava's grip tightened on Samantha's hips, her nails digging into the flesh as she thrust harder and faster. She reveled in the way Samantha's body responded to her, the way she moaned and writhed under her touch.

"Call me Ava," she growled, her voice rough. "And you're going to scream my name."

Samantha's breath hitched at Ava's words. "Fuck me harder," she pleaded, her voice dripping with need. "Make me feel it."

Ava complied, her hips moving in a punishing rhythm that drove Samantha to the brink of sanity. Sweat dripped between them, creating a sticky mess that only added to the sensuality of the moment. Ava licked it off Samantha's neck, tasting the saltiness on her tongue as she ground her hips deeper into Samantha's body.

"Oh god..." Samantha cried out, arching her back in bliss as Ava fucked her brutally. Ava's teeth grazed the soft skin behind Samantha's ear, marking her like an animal claiming its prey. "Fuck... yes!"

Their pace quickened until they both reached another climax together, bodies shuddering convulsively from the force of pleasure coursing through them. Ava cried out, feeling herself explode inside Samantha once more while the futa hunter's walls clamped down around her cock in a tight orgasmic grip.

Their bodies trembled with the force of a supernovae, waves of pleasure crashing over them relentlessly. As their orgasms subsided, Ava collapsed onto Samantha's back, their bodies slick with sweat and the aftermath of their passion. Their heavy breaths filled the room as they lay there in a tangled mess of limbs, basking in the incredible release they had just experienced.

Samantha turned her head to meet Ava's gaze, a smile playing at the corners of her lips. "Damn, I forgot to taste your cock."

Ava grinned. "I am not going anywhere, you know."

Samantha gave Ava's right breast a playful squeeze. "Sorry, I am done for today. But I think I can allow myself a little treat." Her hand reached for Ava's cock, thickly coated in a mix of her sperm and Samantha's juices. Samantha ran her finger along the shaft, collecting the divine liquid, and then sucked the ambrosia off her finger while maintaining eye contact with Ava.

"You're such a tease," Ava laughed. "So maybe I can come tomorrow? Take another look at the pipes you wrecked?"

"Sorry, Ava, but tomorrow I am expecting a guest."

The End.

Futa Hunter: Sultry Escort

Chloe straightened her blouse as she knocked on the hotel room door, preparing to meet her new client. Probably another one of those middle-aged businessmen, eager for an escape from his mundane life for an hour.

The door opened, revealing a stunning young woman with long dark hair and piercing blue eyes. Chloe blinked in surprise, her cheeks flushing. She had never had a female client before.

"You must be Chloe," the woman said with a coy smile. "I'm Samantha. Please, come in."

Chloe hesitated, unsure of how to proceed. Her experience was limited to servicing men, and while she found women attractive, she had never been intimate with one. Still, she was a professional, and she had a job to do. Taking a deep breath, she stepped into the room.

Samantha closed the door behind her, looking Chloe up and down appreciatively. "You're even more gorgeous in person. I've been looking forward to this." She brushed a lock of hair from Chloe's face, her fingertips lingering on Chloe's cheek.

Chloe's breath caught in her throat at Samantha's touch. She cleared her throat, trying to compose herself. "Thank you, but I should clarify that I'm here to pleasure you, not the other way around."

Samantha pouted, stepping closer to Chloe until their bodies nearly touched. "I was hoping we could pleasure each other," she said softly, reaching around to squeeze Chloe's rear.

Chloe gasped, heat flooding between her legs in response. She took a hasty step back, flustered by her body's reaction. "I apologize for the confusion, but I am an escort, not a participant."

"I understand you have a job to do," Samantha said. "But don't you ever get curious what it's like to be with a woman?" She reached for the zipper of Chloe's skirt, slowly drawing it down. "I could show you things you've never even dreamed of."

Samantha spent last two days looking for Chloe on escort websites and now that she finally was here, Samantha was not planning on letting her leave. The moment Samantha saw Chloe picked up by a client near that seedy strip club, she immediately knew that Chloe was an uninitiated futa. Samantha was hunting futas for a long time and she never made mistakes.

Chloe swallowed hard, torn between her duty as an escort and her own simmering curiosity. She had never been with a woman before, though she had certainly thought about it. But this was different—this was work, and she couldn't let herself get distracted.

"I'm afraid I must insist that we stick to the terms of our arrangement," Chloe said, though her voice lacked conviction. She felt helpless under the intensity of Samantha's gaze, pinned in place by eyes that saw far too much.

Samantha smiled, sliding Chloe's skirt down over her hips until it pooled at her feet. "I think we both know you're enjoying this," she purred, trailing a finger down between Chloe's breasts. "Admit it, you're just as curious about me as I am about you. Besides, I am paying you, so you are going to do what I am telling you to do."

Chloe bit her lip, unable to deny the hunger in Samantha's touch or the way her body responded, nipples hardening under her blouse. She had never felt so exposed, stripped bare by Samantha's skillful seduction.

"See?" Samantha whispered, cupping Chloe's cheek. "You want this as much as I do." She kissed Chloe then, a soft press of lips that ignited her blood, and any remaining protests died on Chloe's tongue.

Samantha kissed a path down Chloe's neck as she undid the buttons of her blouse one by one, lavishing praise on each newly revealed inch of skin. "So soft," she murmured, palms skimming over Chloe's stomach. "So perfect." She paused at Chloe's bra, meeting her gaze with a wicked smile. "May I?"

Chloe could only nod, dazed by the riot of sensations flooding her body. She was unused to being undone so thoroughly, but she found she didn't mind—not when it was Samantha doing the undoing.

Samantha unhooked Chloe's bra and slid the straps from her shoulders, leaving her bare from the waist up. She took a step back, eyes dark with desire as they raked over Chloe's figure, and Chloe flushed under the intensity of her admiration.

"Magnificent," Samantha breathed. She reached out to cup Chloe's breasts, thumbs brushing over her nipples, and sparks of pleasure shot through Chloe's body. "Simply magnificent."

Looking at this perfect feminine body and knowing that soon it will be enhanced by a nice thick cock made Samantha wet in an instant.

Samantha kissed and sucked at Chloe's neck as her hands explored lower, pulling down her skirt. "So eager," she purred, palming Chloe's arousal through her panties. "I can feel how much you want this."

Chloe whimpered, caught between the urge to push Samantha away and pull her closer. She had never felt such intense pleasure, and it both thrilled and frightened her. "I don't—I'm not—"

"Shh." Samantha eased Chloe's panties down her legs, leaving her completely bare. "Just feel." She kissed a path down Chloe's body, lavishing attention on her breasts before continuing lower. "You'll understand soon enough."

She settled between Chloe's thighs, hands spreading her open, and Chloe gasped at the first soft stroke of Samantha's tongue. Unfamiliar sensations built within her, pressure and heat that made her thighs tremble, and she leaned against the wall to ground herself as Samantha worked her higher and higher.

"Let go," Samantha urged between strokes of her tongue. "Give in to it."

Chloe shook her head, struggling for coherency. "I can't—it's too much—" The words choked off in a moan as Samantha sucked at her clit, ecstasy engulfing her flesh. But she couldn't go on, something inside of her was changing and she was just too afraid. Chloe tried to push Samantha away and Samantha looked up.

"I know, I know... this is why you became an escort in the first place? You can't have an orgasm because you feel like it will change you and you hate yourself for it. So you thought that becoming an escort will alienate you to sex, but it didn't work... Don't worry, it will all be over soon."

Samantha pinned Chloe's hips in place, denying her escape as she relentlessly drove her pleasure higher. Chloe writhed against the wall, overwhelmed by the intensity of sensation, and when Samantha slid two fingers inside her, she came undone.

A cry tore from her throat as her orgasm crashed over her, wave after wave of bliss that left her trembling and incoherent. She was only dimly aware of something changing within her, a pressure building at her core, and then Samantha was guiding her down to the floor.

"There now," Samantha crooned, stroking Chloe's hair. "Wasn't that wonderful?"

Chloe could only pant for breath, aftershocks still rippling through her. She felt strange, as if her body had been reshaped, and an unfamiliar weight pulled at her groin.

Samantha's hand slid between Chloe's thighs, and she gasped. "Oh!"

Samantha smiled, fingers wrapping around Chloe's new cock. "Welcome to being a futa."

Chloe stared at the enormous appendage jutting from her body, both awed and afraid. She didn't understand how this was possible, yet the sight of it sent a thrill through her, and she moaned as Samantha stroked the sensitive flesh.

"Don't be afraid," Samantha said. "You were made for this. Made to give and receive pleasure in equal measure. And now..." Her hand tightened, twisting in a way that made Chloe cry out. "You get to discover all the pleasures of having a cock."

Chloe swallowed hard, torn between arousal and uncertainty. She had so many questions, but Samantha's ministrations were distracting, drawing her focus to the sensations coursing through her new cock.

"Please," she whimpered, not sure if she was pleading for more or for reprieve.

"Shh." Samantha released her grip, running her hands up and down Chloe's thighs instead. "You'll get used to it. But for now...I want to feel this inside me. You owe me for awakening you and now you will fuck me."

She led Chloe to the bed and pushed her down on the sheets. Samantha undressed herself in hurry, eager to get fucked, exposing her delicious curves and glistening folds. Chloe's eyes were drawn to the sight, her new cock throbbing with anticipation. The mixture of desire and trepidation filled the air as Samantha climbed onto the bed, straddling Chloe's hips.

"Take me," Samantha whispered, her voice thick with need. "Show me what your new cock can do."

Samantha straddled Chloe's hips, positioning her entrance over the tip of Chloe's cock. Chloe stared up at her, wide-eyed, as Samantha slowly sank down, enveloping her in slick heat. They moaned in unison, and Chloe's hands flew to Samantha's hips, clinging for support.

The pleasure was beyond anything she'd experienced before, her cock hypersensitive and attuned to the rhythmic pulses of Samantha's cunt. She rocked experimentally, chasing the sensations, and Samantha grinned down at her.

"That's it," she purred. "Fuck me. I want to feel you come inside me."

Arousal and power surged through Chloe, and she thrust up into Samantha without thinking. Samantha cried out, nails digging into Chloe's shoulders, and heat flooded Chloe's senses.

Chloe's heart raced as she watched Samantha's chest heave with each thrust, her tight pussy clamping down on Chloe's invading cock. It felt so good, yet it was overwhelming. She was no longer just getting fucked, but now she was the one doing the fucking. The sweat dripping from both of their bodies mixed together, adding an unexpectedly tangy taste to the air, and Chloe writhed beneath Samantha with every powerful thrust. The bed squeaked in protest and Samantha hissed through her teeth every time Chloe bottomed out inside her, gripping the sheets with determination.

"Fuck! Yes! Give it to me!" Samantha cried out, her eyes rolling back into her head as she sought release from Chloe's skilled ministrations. Chloe could feel the tension building within Samantha's body; she didn't know how to deal with it, but she wanted this woman to cum. They moved together now, finding a rhythm that had them both moaning and grunting with pleasure.

Chloe's cock throbbed in anticipation as they locked eyes, sharing a primal connection only heightened by their newfound passion for one another's bodies.

Samantha gripped Chloe's shoulders firmly and leaned forward, pressing their lips together in a searing kiss that left them both breathless. Her tongue invaded Chloe's mouth hungrily before she broke away with a gasp. "I'm close," she panted against Chloe's lips, "so fucking close. Fuck me harder, now!"

Chloe didn't know how and why, but she knew exactly what to do, as if she was born with a cock. How to thrust, how to move her glutes the right way, where to place her feet for better support, it all came naturally to her as she grabbed Samantha's ass and began fucking her from below like there was no tomorrow.

Samantha swiveled her hips, grinding against Chloe's thick shaft as it filled her up. Her eyes rolled into the back of her head and a moan ripped from her lips as Chloe could feel Samantha's cunt clench around her cock, pulling on it hungrily, begging for more as she pumped into her. She rode out the wave of pleasure, feeling Samantha's body shudder beneath hers. Their kisses were fierce and demanding, tongues dueling as they explored each other's mouths.

Chloe's face flushed crimson from exertion and arousal, strands of saliva connecting them as they gazed into each other's eyes as they fucked like dirty animals.

Samantha's body shook as she climaxed, screaming Chloe's name. Her hot walls pulsing around Chloe's cock, milking every last drop of pleasure from her futa lover. Her fingers digging into Chloe's shoulders, her nails leaving crescents of pain that turned into pleasure as they pushed her over the edge. Chloe's entire body tensed up, and with a loud moan, she too came, filling Samantha's cunt with hot semen. They both cried out in unison, their mouths crashing together in a passionate kiss. Their tongues danced wildly, exploring each other's mouths as they rode out the waves of pleasure.

As they came down from their high, their heavy breathing slowed down gradually. Chloe couldn't quite believe what just happened. She looked down between them, seeing her own cum leaking out of Samantha's pussy and forming a tiny puddle on the sheets. They were both covered in sweat and moisture, their bodies glistening under the dim room lights. Samantha smiled up at her before pulling away to rest her forehead against Chloe's. "That," she breathed out softly, "was incredible."

Chloe looked at Samantha, taking in the lust-filled eyes and flushed skin. They lay there together, their hearts pounding in sync as they tried to catch their breath.

For a long moment, they stayed locked together. Chloe's cock was still hard inside Samantha, desire not yet sated, but she felt overwhelmed and adrift.

Samantha cupped her face, gazing down at her with a possessive sort of affection. "My sweet futa," she murmured. "You were made for this."

Chloe swallowed, unsure but unable to deny the truth in Samantha's words. She had been remade, and there was no going back.

Samantha rose up, sliding off Chloe's cock with a wet sound, and Chloe whimpered at the loss. But Samantha only smiled, shifting to straddle Chloe's waist, the slick heat of her cunt pressed to Chloe's stomach.

"Samantha, why I am still hard?"

"Because you are a futa. Laws of men don't apply to you, both literally and metaphorically. So, ready for more?" she purred, rolling her hips. Chloe could only nod, mouth dry, as Samantha lifted up and sank back down onto her cock in one smooth glide.

The pleasure was blinding, and Chloe cried out, hands flying to Samantha's hips again. Samantha rode her in earnest now, breasts bouncing, head thrown back in ecstasy, and Chloe could only stare up at her, dazed and awestruck.

Samantha was a goddess, powerful and demanding, and Chloe was putty in her hands. She moved as Samantha directed, chasing her pleasure, fucking up into Samantha's willing body. Her whole world narrowed to the slick clutch of Samantha's cunt and the ache in her cock, building and building.

Samantha leaned down and Chloe felt her hot breath on her ear. "This was just a tease. Now you will repay me properly."

Chloe growled and pushed Samantha off her body.

Chloe gripped Samantha's hips, flipping her over onto her back and pinning her wrists above her head. A predatory hunger burned in her eyes as she positioned herself between Samantha's legs. Samantha looked up at her, excitement and desire shimmering in her gaze. "Show me what you can do," she breathed, anticipation lacing her words.

Chloe's futa cock throbbed, demanding release, as she leaned down to capture Samantha's lips in a scorching kiss. The taste of their mingled desire filled her mouth as tongues battled for dominance.

With a swift movement, Chloe released Samantha's hands and trailed her fingers down her lover's body, tracing the curve of her breasts and the dip of her waist. Samantha arched into the touch, moaning softly, the sound spurring Chloe on. She continued her exploration, sliding her fingers lower until she reached Samantha's core.

Samantha gasped as Chloe's skilled fingers found their mark, stroking and teasing her swollen clit. She writhed beneath Chloe, hips grinding against her hand in an urgent rhythm. Chloe watched, captivated by the sight of Samantha losing control under her touch.

But Chloe wanted more—and so she thrust forward, burying herself deep inside Samantha's pusst. Samantha gasped at the sudden intrusion, arching her back and gripping the sheets beneath her. Chloe set a relentless pace, her thrusts hard and fast, each one driving them both closer to the edge. She reveled in the power she had over Samantha, relishing in the way her body writhed beneath hers.

Their bodies moved together in perfect synchrony, a dance of passion and desire. Chloe's grip on Samantha's hips tightened as she pounded into her with unbridled force.

Samantha moaned, digging her nails into Chloe's flesh as she felt herself being filled once more. Their hips slapped together in rhythm, creating an echoing smack against the bed. Chloe's cock stretched Samantha's walls and hit a spot deep inside of her that made her toes curl, sending a rush of pleasure through her body. The room filled with the sounds of skin slapping against skin, of grunts and moans, of wet noises as their bodies moved together with animalistic fervor.

Chloe leaned down to capture Samantha's lips in a fierce kiss, her tongue fighting for ecstasy within the confines of their heated mouths. She breathed heavily against Samantha's lips while thrusting deeper, feeling the warmth surround her throbbing cock with each plunge. Her free hand found its way between them, rubbing Samantha's clit roughly, causing her lover to buck her hips up to meet Chloe's thrusts.

Samantha broke the kiss, panting heavily as she arched her back off the mattress. "Fuck," she groaned. She stared up at Chloe with lust-filled eyes that sparkled with desire. "Don't stop."

Another wave of pleasure washed over Samantha as Chloe's cock twitched inside of her, pulling out and thrusting back in harder than before. She could feel herself getting closer and closer to the edge; she dug her nails into Chloe's shoulders again as she rode out the sensation. No matter how many times Samantha did, getting fucked by a virgin futa was the most exquisite pleasure.

This is why she did what she did, why futa hunting was her hobby, her job, her way of life.

With a primal growl, Chloe gave in to her instincts and began to piston her hips, relentlessly driving into Samantha's body, her cock stretching the tight cunt as she found a rhythm that left them both gasping. Her thrusts were confident now, echoing against the mattress as she claimed Samantha's body once more. She leaned down, capturing Samantha's lips in another scorching kiss, their tongues twisting together as their passion ignited once more. The taste of their combined arousal only fueled her lust, spurring her on to drive deeper inside of Samantha with every stroke.

Samantha's hands clenched into fists as she met Chloe's movements, pushing back against each forceful plunge. Her breasts bounced with every thud of their hips, chest heaving in time with Chloe's frantic pace. She moaned around their kiss, and Chloe groaned in response, feeling the walls of her cunt clenching around Chloe's shaft. Their bodies slid against each other, slick with sweat and sex as they moved in unison.

Samantha broke away from the kiss with a needy gasp, looking at Chloe with eyes full of desire. "Fuck," she breathed out, "you feel so good." The words left her mouth in a mix of wanton lust and admiration for this woman who had taken control so effortlessly. She arched her back off the mattress as Chloe picked up the pace even more, hitting that perfect spot inside her over and over again.

Chloe grinned. "It feels so good to fuck, to have a cock. Is this how men feel?"

Samantha laughed. "Forget about men. You are unique, exquisite, this is your nature."

Samantha's body trembled beneath Chloe's relentless assault, her moans growing louder with each thrust. She clawed at the sheets, losing herself in the overwhelming sensations that consumed her. Her walls clenched around Chloe's cock, urging her on, begging for release.

Chloe could feel the coil of pleasure tightening in her groin, building up with an intensity that threatened to consume her entirely. The room was filled with the symphony of their cries and the intoxicating scent of their desire. Samantha's body was a canvas for Chloe's desires, a playground for them to explore.

As Chloe continued to fuck Samantha with unyielding determination, she leaned down to capture one of Samantha's hardened nipples between her lips. She suckled and licked, bit and teased, until her cock exploded with cum right inside Samantha's cunt. The pulsating waves of pleasure washed over Chloe as she released herself inside Samantha, the intense sensation rocking her body to its core. Samantha's walls clenched around Chloe's cock, sucking every drop of release from her, amplifying their pleasure. Chloe's breath hitched as she collapsed onto Samantha, their bodies entwined in a post-orgasmic embrace.

This time Samantha gave Chloe no time to rest. Her lips wrapped around Chloe's cock, thickly coated with a mix of her own juices and Chloe's cum, as the same cocktail of sex slowly oozed out of her own glistening pussy. Samantha's fingers made their way to Chloe's wet cunt and penetrated it once again, and the dual sensations drove Chloe insane.

Samantha's hot breath felt like a flame on Chloe's skin as she suckled on her sensitive flesh, causing Chloe to shiver and moan in response. Her fingers thrust recklessly into Chloe's wet folds as she dove into her core.

Samantha slurped on Chloe's cum as she sucked faster and faster, in rhythm with the movement of her fingers. Chloe's body trembled under Samantha's expert touch, her senses overwhelmed by the ecstasy coursing through her veins. She gripped the sheets tightly, arching her back as a wave of pleasure crashed over her. Samantha's fingers worked tirelessly, plunging in and out of Chloe's wetness, each stroke driving her closer to the edge.

Samantha sucked with abandon, her cheeks hollowing out with every movement of her head. Chloe's moans grew louder, filling the room with the symphony of their pleasure. Samantha could feel the tension building within Chloe's body, a telltale sign that she was on the precipice of orgasm. Samantha could sense Chloe's impending orgasm, and she intensified her efforts.

Suddenly, Chloe grabbed Samantha by the hair and pulled out of her mouth. "No, I want more."

Chloe pinned Samantha against the bed and Samantha filled the tip of Chloe's cock brushing against her forbidden entrance. "Wait, wrong hole!"

Chloe grinned. "No, this is the right hole."

Chloe buried herself to the hilt in Samantha's ass in a second and Samantha cried out in pain and pleasure. The sudden intrusion sent a wave of mixed sensations coursing through Samantha's body. The burn of stretching against her tight ring mingled with the electrifying pleasure that pulsed through her core. She gasped, her breath hitching as Chloe's thick cock filled her ass completely.

Chloe paused, holding herself still inside Samantha, giving her time to adjust to the new sensation. Samantha's body trembled beneath her, a mixture of pain and desire evident in her eyes. Chloe leaned down, pressing gentle kisses along Samantha's neck, whispering soothing words to ease her discomfort.

"Is this enough for you," Chloe whispered, her voice trembling with lust. "Is my debt paid in full?"

Samantha shook her head. "No," she said firmly. "Cream my ass, and then we are even."

Chloe slowly began to move her hips, withdrawing almost completely before thrusting back in with deliberate force.

Samantha let out a guttural moan, the initial discomfort giving way to a heady pleasure that enveloped her senses. The burning sensation transformed into an intoxicating mix of pain and ecstasy as Chloe filled her thoroughly, each powerful thrust pushing her closer to the edge. She braced herself against the mattress, fingers gripping the sheets tightly as she surrendered to the overwhelming pleasure.

Chloe's movements grew more confident and calculated, finding a rhythm that left them both breathless. As she delved deeper into Samantha's ass, she could feel the tightness gradually giving way to accommodate her girth.

Samantha's face scrunched up as Chloe's cock stretched her ass with every thrust. The feeling of being filled to the brim was both exhilarating and terrifying, sending shockwaves of desire coursing through her body. She moaned loudly, unable to hide her desire from Chloe as the tight walls of her asshole began to relax around the invader's cock.

Chloe groaned, loving the sight of Samantha squirming beneath her. "You look so good when you're mine," she whispered against Samantha's ear before kissing it softly. Her hips picked up their pace, driving in and out of her lover's ass with more force than before. Every movement sent delicious tremors through Samantha's body, causing her to arch her back off the mattress in ecstasy.

Samantha's mind was lost in a haze of pleasure and need, her fingers digging into the sheets as she tried to find purchase against the torrent of sensation crashing over her. With each thrust from Chloe, Samantha felt herself getting closer to the edge once again.

She could feel the coil of pleasure winding tighter and tighter within her, ready to explode in a breathtaking climax. Every stroke of Chloe's cock inside her ass sent shockwaves of pleasure radiating through her body, electrifying her senses.

Chloe's grip on Samantha's waist tightened as she pounded into her ass with relentless determination. The sounds of their bodies colliding mixed with the symphony of their moans, filling the room with raw desire. Samantha's body quivered beneath Chloe's unyielding assault, the pleasure becoming too much to bear. Samantha's body tensed as Chloe's thrusts became harder, faster. Her mind was consumed by the overwhelming pleasure, her thoughts reduced to a single mantra: Chloe, Chloe, Chloe.

With one final thrust, Chloe buried herself deep within Samantha's ass and held her in place, as if marking her territory.

Samantha's vision blurred as wave after wave of pleasure crashed over her, the intensity building within her core. Her whole body shook as she succumbed to the rapture, her release washing over her like a tidal wave. She let out a primal scream, her voice mingling with Chloe's own cries of satisfaction.

Chloe drank in Samantha's pleasure, relishing in the way Samantha's body clenched around her cock. The tightness and warmth of Samantha's ass pushed Chloe to the brink of her own orgasm.

With a guttural groan, Chloe reached her peak, her orgasm crashing over her like a tidal wave. She released herself deep inside Samantha's ass, filling her to the brim with her hot seed. Chloe's hips continued to piston into Samantha's ass, the friction sending electrifying pleasure coursing through her body as she emptied herself again and again inside Samantha's forbidden tunnel.

As the waves of pleasure subsided, Chloe slowly withdrew from Samantha's ass, her heart pounding in her chest. They lay side by side on the bed, bodies glistening with sweat and tangled in a mess of sheets. Samantha's fingers traced lazy patterns along Chloe's arm, her touch sending shivers down Chloe's spine.

"I think I am done for today. So how much do I owe you," Samantha whispered.

Chloe smiled softly. "Keep your money, silly. By the way, what are you doing tomorrow, can I come over?"

"Sorry, but no. Tomorrow I am going to a fashion show."

The End.

Futa Hunter: Snobby Supermodel

The crimson silk of Samantha's dress clung to her like a second skin, the fabric accentuating every dip and curve of her sexy form as she sauntered into the fashion show. Eyes followed her, drawn by the audacious display of confidence and unabashed sexuality. She took her seat in the front row, an arm's length from the runway where beauty incarnate would parade before hungry gazes.

"Darling, you look ravishing," cooed a voice nearby, its owner bathed in the soft glow of admiration. Samantha turned, her piercing blue eyes locking onto her friend Lisa, the architect behind this night of glamour.

"Thank you, sweetie. I wouldn't miss your big night for the world," Samantha replied.

As the lights dimmed and the first model emerged, draped in layers of chiffon and lace that fluttered with each poised step, Samantha's attention was partially on the cascade of fabrics—exquisite manifestations of haute couture—but her mind was elsewhere, senses on alert. Then she saw her: Victoria James. The supermodel commanded the podium, wrapped in an avant-garde ensemble that hugged her lithe frame, the vibrant hues of the garment playing off her wavy brown hair and hazel eyes that spoke volumes of untold secrets.

"Isn't she something?" Samantha murmured to Lisa, her eyes never leaving Victoria's figure as it sashayed with a grace that seemed almost otherworldly.

"Victoria? A goddess among mortals," her friend agreed, blissfully unaware of the undercurrents swirling within Samantha's thoughts. "Came out of nowhere, skyrocketed to the top."

There it was—the telltale sign. Only Samantha could discern the subtle fluidity in Victoria's movements, the poise that was more than just practiced elegance. It was a silent siren call to someone like Samantha—a futa hunter. And Samantha, she was never wrong.

"Can you get me her contact info? For... networking purposes," Samantha said casually, though her heart thrummed with the excitement of the chase.

"Of course, I have her details right here," Lisa replied, tapping away at her smartphone, oblivious to the hunt that had just begun.

As the digits appeared on Samantha's screen, her lips curled into a smile that promised sin and salvation all at once. Each fashion show was a feast for the eyes, but this one had presented an unexpected delicacy. Her pulse quickened; even after all these years, the thrill of awakening another futa surged through her like a first kiss—intoxicating, frightening, and utterly irresistible.

"Thank you, darling. You're an angel," Samantha purred, pocketing her phone. Her mind was already crafting the web that would ensnare the exquisite Victoria James, and her body hummed in anticipation of the pleasure that would unfurl from the conquest.

"Anything for you. Enjoy the rest of the show," her friend said, beaming at Samantha before turning back to the spectacle of fashion and flesh.

Samantha settled back into her chair, her gaze fixed on Victoria as she owned the runway, basking in the adulation of the crowd. The supermodel might've been oblivious to her nature, but soon enough, she would unravel beneath Samantha's touch, and her true essence would be unveiled. Samantha could hardly wait.

***

The evening sky bled into dusky purples and blues as Samantha Carter arrived home, the adrenaline from the fashion show still coursing through her veins. She kicked off her heels, their clatter echoing in the spacious apartment as she eyed her newest acquisition: a high-end camera resting atop its box like an offering to her mission. Its sleek black body gleamed under the soft lights, but it was the thick manual that lay beside it that truly held her attention.

"Right," she muttered to herself, flicking through the dense pages. "Aperture, ISO, shutter speed... How hard can it be?" Her fingers danced over the buttons and dials, memorizing their locations, learning the language of photography with a fervor fueled by more than just artistic passion.

Hours dissolved into minutes, and as midnight approached, Samantha's fingers paused over her smartphone, poised to weave her web. With a sly smile, she opened Victoria James' social media profile and began drafting her message. Every word was chosen with care, designed to intrigue and entice.

"Dear Victoria," she typed, "Your presence on the runway today was nothing short of captivating. I'm an exclusive photographer looking to capture your ethereal beauty in a private shoot. Unfortunately, my scheduled model has taken ill, and I find myself in need of someone who embodies grace and elegance. Would you honor me with your participation tomorrow? By the way, Lisa said hi."

She hit 'send' before she could second guess herself, and as the digital missive flew into the ether, she felt the familiar thrill of the hunt pulse within her.

The response came sooner than expected. Victoria's words popped up on the screen, their tone laced with the supermodel's characteristic confidence. "That sounds delightful. I'd love to. When and where?"

"Perfect," Samantha whispered, her eyes glinting with triumph. The pieces were falling into place.

***

The studio was an intimate affair, with high ceilings and white walls that seemed to wait expectantly for creativity to fill their blankness. Samantha had arranged a few lights and reflectors—mere window dressing to the untrained eye, but to her, they were props in the theater of seduction.

Victoria arrived on time, her tall frame wrapped in a casual chic ensemble that contrasted sharply with the image of perfection she presented on the catwalk. She scanned the room, taking in the lack of personnel and the meager setup with a raised eyebrow.

"Working solo today?" Victoria inquired.

"Always," Samantha lied smoothly, stepping closer to Victoria with the confidence of a seasoned artist. "I find it creates a better connection between the subject and the lens. Just you, me, and the camera. It's pure."

"Interesting philosophy." Victoria's gaze lingered on Samantha, appraising. "No assistants bustling about, no stylists fussing over every strand of hair... it's certainly... unique."

"Unique is what I strive for," Samantha replied, allowing the corner of her mouth to quirk up playfully. "You'll see. The results will be stunning."

"Alright then." Victoria's hesitation melted into a smirk. "Let's make some art."

"You know, Victoria, the camera can only capture what's already there—and you'll make my job easy."

"Flattery will get you everywhere, Ms. Photographer," Victoria teased back, her hazel eyes sparkling.

"Call me Samantha," she said, closing in just enough to let her breath brush against Victoria's ear. "And trust me, I plan to go everywhere."

Victoria's laughter filled the space, warm and genuine. She leaned in, her breath now mingling with Samantha's, their proximity blurring professional lines. "Then lead the way, Samantha."

***

The shutter snapped shut with a sharp click, echoing through the semi-barren studio as Samantha coaxed Victoria into yet another captivating pose. "Gorgeous," she murmured, eyes locked on the viewfinder while her subject arched gracefully under the spotlight—a siren bathed in soft luminescence. "Now, let's lose the jacket; I want to capture the elegance of your shoulders."

"Direct and daring," Victoria commented, letting the fabric slide off her skin with a practiced ease, her eyes never leaving Samantha's. "I like that."

"Good," Samantha said with a low chuckle, her blue eyes twinkling with mischief. She advanced a step, camera momentarily forgotten at her side. "Because there's plenty more where that came from."

Victoria posed, the camera shutter capturing every subtle shift of her lithe figure. Yet as the session unfolded, the supermodel's keen gaze caught the slight fumbling of Samantha's fingers on the camera dials, the hesitant adjustment of the lens. A crease formed between Victoria's brows.

"Stop there," Victoria commanded suddenly, hands on her hips. Her smirk had waned, replaced by a shrewdness that cut through her earlier playfulness. "Samantha, is it? Do you actually know what you're doing with that thing?"

"Absolutely," Samantha shot back, though her heart skipped a beat. Tossing her hair over her shoulder, she stepped closer, feeling the heat of Victoria's body even without touching. "I'm capturing your essence—the raw beauty that others can only dream of framing."

"Flattery again," Victoria quipped, but her tone held an edge. She eyed the camera, then met Samantha's piercing gaze. "But my 'essence' isn't going to look good if the person behind the camera doesn't know how to light me properly. This angle is all wrong, and you've barely adjusted the settings since we started."

Samantha's pulse quickened. The ruse was slipping, the huntress teetering on the brink of exposure. With a confidence she didn't fully feel, she lowered the camera, her lips curling into a suggestive smile. "Maybe I'm just more interested in other... angles."

"Is that so?" Victoria's skepticism was palpable, but her curiosity seemed piqued. She took a step forward, closing the gap until they were mere inches apart. "Tell me, 'Ms. Photographer,' what exactly were you hoping to shoot today?"

"Something breathtaking," Samantha whispered, locking eyes with Victoria. Her breath hitched as she drank in the sight of the supermodel—this goddess of fashion, standing vulnerable and questioning before her.

"Guess we'll see about that," Victoria murmured, her voice a mix of challenge and intrigue. She didn't step back, didn't break the connection. Instead, she waited—for clarification, for the next move, for the truth.

Samantha's mind raced, instincts clashing against desire. Admitting the truth now could ruin everything, yet lying felt like squandering this electric moment. She needed to navigate this carefully—after all, the true art of the hunt was not in the kill, but in the seductive dance that led to surrender.

"I confess I only wanted to seduce you and fuck your brains out," Samantha said, her piercing blue eyes gazing into Victoria's.

Victoria laughed, a throaty chuckle that sent a shiver of delight down Samantha's spine. "My, my, aren't you bold," Victoria purred. "Most men just offer me money or send dick pics. You actually put in effort. I like that."

Samantha's heart raced. Victoria wasn't repulsed. In fact, she seemed intrigued. "I've always been curious about women," Victoria admitted. "And you are rather stunning. So, why the hell not?"

Samantha wasted no time. She pulled Victoria close, caressing her lithe body as their lips met in a passionate kiss. Victoria's tongue danced with hers, and Samantha groaned. She slid her hands under Victoria's silk blouse, fingers teasing her erect nipples.

Victoria gasped, breaking the kiss. "More," she whispered huskily. "I want more."

Grinning, Samantha sank to her knees. She slid Victoria's skirt and panties down her long, shapely legs, drinking in the sight of Victoria's glistening sex.

Soon, very soon there will be a huge cock for Samantha to suck, but her cunt will do for now.

Samantha leaned in, inhaling Victoria's musky scent before swiping her tongue along Victoria's slit.

Victoria cried out, tangling her fingers in Samantha's hair. Samantha lapped at Victoria's clit before thrusting two fingers inside her, stroking in time with the rhythm of her tongue. Victoria bucked against her, fucking herself on Samantha's fingers as her moans grew louder and more desperate.

"Oh God, don't stop!" Victoria shrieked. Samantha increased her pace, curling her fingers to stroke Victoria's sweet spot.

Victoria climaxed with a scream, her inner walls clenching around Samantha's fingers.

And then Victoria's eyes widened as a bulge formed under her skin right above her clit. She glanced down with a mix of shock and awe, watching as her new cock erupted outside her body.

"What's happening to me?" Victoria asked, her voice trembling.

Samantha smiled, running her hands along Victoria's length. "You're awakening, my dear. Becoming who you were always meant to be. A futa."

Victoria gasped as Samantha stroked her, sensations unlike anything she'd experienced before flooding her body. Her cock grew harder and larger under Samantha's expert touch until it sprang free to it's full size, jutting out from Victoria's body.

"You see?" Samantha purred. "You were made for this."

Victoria stared at her new appendage, stunned into silence. Her cock felt so natural, like it had always been a part of her. Yet she'd lived over twenty years without it.

Samantha guided Victoria's hands to her cock, showing her how to pleasure herself. "Futas like us were born to give and receive pleasure in equal measure. Your cock will be a source of delight for both you and your partners."

"Partners?" Victoria squeaked.

"Of course." Samantha stroked Victoria's length, pulling a groan from her. "Once you've learned to master your new gift, you'll find lovers begging for a taste of what you offer. But first..." She sank to her knees, gazing up at Victoria with a wicked gleam in her eyes. "You owe me payment for your awakening."

Victoria's eyes darkened with lust. She fisted her cock, rubbing the tip along Samantha's lips. "On your knees then, Ms. Photographer. And open wide."

The studio lights beat down on their naked, gorgeous bodies. Samantha's hands roamed over Victoria's flawless skin, tracing the contours of her hips, her breasts, the valley between her legs.

Samantha's lips curled into a knowing smile, her piercing blue eyes locking onto Victoria's. "You are the best of both worlds," she purred, sliding a finger between Victoria's folds. Victoria gasped, hips jerking forward to seek more of that delicious friction. "I'm going to make you feel so good."

Victoria could only moan in response, hands clenching at her sides.

Samantha chuckled, clearly reading her hesitation. "Relax," she said, taking Victoria's cock into her mouth, enveloping the sensitive organ in wet heat.

A strangled cry escaped Victoria's lips. It felt so good, almost too good. She tangled her hands in Samantha's hair, torn between pulling her closer and pushing her away.

Samantha looked up at her through lowered lashes, blue eyes gleaming with lust and triumph. She sucked hard on Victoria's cock, hollowing her cheeks, and Victoria lost the battle with herself.

"Oh God," she moaned, grip tightening in Samantha's hair. "Just like that, don't stop..."

Samantha purred around her length, the vibrations shooting straight to Victoria's core as she slid another finger into Victoria's pussy, curling them upwards to stroke that sensitive spot inside her. Victoria cried out, back arching off the table as her inner walls clenched around Samantha's fingers.

"So wet for me," Samantha purred, withdrawing her fingers only to thrust them back in. She sucked Victoria's cock in time with her fingers, bringing Victoria to the brink of orgasm again and again only to pull back at the last second.

"Please," Victoria whimpered, beyond caring how wanton she sounded. She needed release, needed Samantha to give her what she so desperately craved.

"What do you need, Victoria?" Samantha asked, her breath ghosting over Victoria's slick cock. "Tell me."

"I need to come," Victoria said, cheeks flaming. "Please let me come, Samantha, I can't take anymore!"

"As you wish," Samantha said, and then she was swallowing Victoria's cock once again, her cheeks hollowing as she sucked with fervor. Samantha's nimble fingers dove in deeper, stroking, teasing the sweet spot inside Victoria's dripping cunt.

Victoria screamed out in pleasure, her nails digging into Samantha's shoulders as her body convulsed wildly. "Fuck, Sam!" she cried out, the sensation of Samantha's mouth and fingers working together was too much for her. She came hard, squirting onto Samantha's fingers that continued to stroke her through her climax and erupted into Samantha's mouth at the same time.

Victoria's first ejaculation felt divine as she unloaded cum into Samantha's mouth. The climax hit with the force of an avalanche, sweeping over Victoria in wave after crashing wave. She screamed Samantha's name, hips bucking against her lover's mouth as she came.

Samantha didn't let up until Victoria was spent, every last drop of fresh sperm milked from her body. Only then did Samantha raise her head, smirking at the dazed expression on Victoria's face.

Their heavy breathing filled the room as they collapsed onto the floor together. Samantha cuddled up next to Victoria whose chest still heaved from the intensity of her orgasm.

"Welcome to your new reality," Samantha whispered, tracing lazy circles around Victoria's still hard cock.

Victoria could do nothing but nod, her mind still reeling from what had happened. She looked down at herself, at the new appendage that was now a part of her body. It felt natural yet strange all at once.

"What now?" she asked quietly.

"Now," Samantha said with a soft smile. "Now, you fuck me. One perk of being a futa is that you don't need to recharge, so come on, on your back!"

With that, Samantha pushed Victoria down and straddled her, sliding onto Victoria's cock in one smooth motion, enveloping her in silken heat. Victoria cried out, back arching as she was finally, blissfully sheathed inside Samantha's welcoming body.

Samantha rode her hard and fast, one hand working between her legs as the other groped her own breasts.

"That is incredible," Samantha groaned, riding fast and hard. "You were made for this, Victoria. Your cock is a work of art."

Victoria clenched her jaw, attempting to hold back the rising wave of pleasure. The sight of Samantha writhing on top of her, flushed and panting, drove every sexual instinct in her wild.

Victoria watched in mute fascination as Samantha rode her. Her hands moved of their own accord, reaching up to cup Samantha's ample breasts, thumbing over her nipples until they were hard and peaked.

"Oh, Victoria," Samantha purred, her hips moving rhythmically against Victoria's as she captured one of Victoria's hands to guide it towards her own center. She was wet and warm and so very inviting; it made Victoria ache with a need she'd never felt before.

The sensation was unlike anything Victoria had ever experienced. She had been on the receiving end of such pleasure before, but giving it was an entirely different matter. Victoria clenched her jaw, attempting to hold back the rising wave of pleasure. The sight of Samantha writhing on top of her, flushed and panting, drove every sexual instinct in her wild.

"Sam," she gasped, hands gripping Samantha's hips to guide her movements. "You're... you're amazing."

Samantha merely laughed, a rich and velvety sound that seemed to vibrate through Victoria's body. She clenched around Victoria's cock, causing the latter to throw her head back with a moan.

"I can feel you," Samantha cooed, leaning forward so her breasts brushed against Victoria's own. "You're so hard for me. You want to come inside me, don't you?"

"Yes," Victoria breathed out, straining against the pleasure that tightened around her like a coil. "Yes, please..."

Samantha smirked, grinding down onto Victoria one final time before driving herself upwards.

"Come for me," Samantha panted, inner walls clenching around Victoria's length. "Come inside me, Victoria, I want to feel you fill me up!"

That did it. With a strangled cry, Victoria came harder than she ever had before, spilling herself inside Samantha's eager body. Samantha followed soon after, inner walls milking every last drop from Victoria as her own orgasm overtook her.

They collapsed together in a tangle of limbs, Victoria still nestled inside Samantha's warmth.

Samantha rolled off of Victoria with a satisfied sigh, Victoria's cock slipping free of her body. Victoria moaned at the loss, already craving the intimacy of their joining again.

"That was divine," Samantha purred, tracing idle patterns over Victoria's sweat-slicked skin.

Victoria blushed, unsure how to respond to such frank praise. "I—thank you," she said. "You were amazing as well. I've never felt anything like that before."

"I told you I'd awaken something special in you," Samantha said smugly. She leaned in to kiss Victoria, slow and deep, and Victoria could taste herself on Samantha's lips. "Are you ready to explore more?"

Victoria swallowed hard, anticipation and nerves warring in her belly. "What did you have in mind?"

Samantha's grin turned wicked. "I want to feel this gorgeous cock of yours in my ass," she purred. "I want you to fuck me until I can't walk straight, Victoria. Are you up for the challenge?"

Just the thought was enough to have Victoria's cock get even harder, and she groaned in response. She knew it would be an experience like no other, and she found herself nodding before she could think better of it.

Samantha rewarded her with another searing kiss. "That's my girl. Now, get behind me and grab my hips. Go slowly, let me guide you in." She got on her hands and knees, presenting herself to Victoria in offering.

Heart hammering, Victoria positioned herself behind Samantha, cock in hand as she stared at Samantha's pink, puckered hole. This was yet another first, but if it was anything like their previous joining, Victoria knew she was in for the ride of her life. She steeled her nerves and began to press forward, encouraged by Samantha's throaty moans.

The head of Victoria's cock breached Samantha's entrance, and they both gasped. Victoria froze, overwhelmed by the incredible tightness and heat enveloping just the tip of her length.

"So good," Samantha breathed, rocking back onto Victoria's cock and drawing her in a little more. "Keep going, Victoria, you feel amazing. Stretch me open on that perfect cock of yours!"

Emboldened, Victoria continued her steady push forward, groaning as she sank deeper and deeper into Samantha's ass. The feeling was indescribable, and Victoria knew she wouldn't last long in the face of such intense pleasure.

When her hips were finally flush against Samantha's ass, they both shuddered in bliss. Samantha's hole gripped Victoria like a vice, rippling around her length as Samantha adjusted to being so fully filled.

"Move," Samantha ordered, voice ragged. "Fuck me, Victoria, just like I taught you. Make me yours!"

Victoria drew back and thrust forward, burying herself to the hilt in Samantha's forbidden hole. Samantha cried out in pleasure, and Victoria began to move in earnest, overcome by the primal need to claim Samantha for her own.

She pounded into Samantha's ass with abandon, her harsh breaths and the slap of skin on skin filling the room. Samantha was nearly screaming beneath her, begging for more, harder and faster. Victoria obliged, chasing her own climax as she strove to bring Samantha the same ecstasy.

When Samantha came with a wail, Victoria followed close behind. She spilled deep within Samantha's ass, hips jerking erratically as her orgasm overtook her.

Utterly spent, they collapsed to the floor together. Victoria's cock slipped free of Samantha's abused hole, and Samantha whimpered at the loss.

"Incredible," Samantha breathed, eyes shining as she looked at Victoria. "You were made for this, Victoria, just like I told you. My perfect little futa, all mine to play with."

"Fuck, I can't believe I am doing this. This is surreal."

Samantha purred in satisfaction, running her hands possessively over Victoria's sweat-slicked body. "This is more than real. Ready for more, my darling futa?"

Victoria shivered, because she was more than ready.

Samantha's grin was predatory as she pushed Victoria onto her back once more and straddled her hips. She gripped Victoria's still-hard cock and guided it to her dripping cunt, sinking down with a throaty moan.

Victoria gasped, hands flying to Samantha's hips. The sensation of that velvet heat enveloping her oversensitive cock was almost too much to bear.

But Samantha gave her no time to adjust, already undulating atop her in a steady rhythm. Victoria cried out, torn between pleasure and discomfort, but Samantha ignored her plaintive sounds, focused only on her own pleasure.

Victoria's cock twitched inside Samantha's cunt, betraying her arousal despite the almost painful stimulation. Samantha leaned down, her full breasts brushing against Victoria's chest as she purred, "You love this, don't you? Being used for my pleasure, giving me everything I desire."

Her rhythm increased, and Victoria gave herself over to the dual sensations of discomfort and ecstasy, finding her pleasure in Samantha's greedy moans and the clenching heat of her cunt.

When Samantha came with a scream, Victoria followed close behind, spilling deep inside her. Samantha collapsed atop her, both of them panting harshly.

"Perfect," Samantha whispered, pressing a kiss to Victoria's throat. "My perfect little futa."

Victoria could only cling to her, drunk on pleasure and devotion.

They lay together for a long while, limbs entangled and hearts slowing to a contented rhythm. Eventually, Samantha rolled onto her side, trailing her fingers down Victoria's chest in a possessive caress.

"I think that's enough for today," she said softly. "I am getting tired."

Victoria shivered, her cock still hard. "What about tomorrow?" she whispered.

Samantha's smile was slow and predatory. "Sorry, but tomorrow I have an appointment with a doctor."

The End.

Futa Hunter: Dirty Doctor

Samantha Carter stepped through the frosted glass door of Dr. Emily Parker's office, a concoction of anxiety and excitement bubbling within her like a wicked potion. Her heart thrummed against her ribcage, not from the faux pains she claimed to suffer but from the anticipation of the hunt. Dr. Emily Parker, unaware of her dormant futa nature, was about to be awakened.

Samantha was a futa hunter and she was good at this.

"Good afternoon, you must be Samantha," Emily greeted, her voice as soothing as the warm hues of her office. The walls were adorned with diplomas that spoke of hard-won knowledge, and bookshelves brimming with medical texts cast an intellectual aura over the room.

"Nice to meet you, Doctor," Samantha began, her tone laced with feigned distress, "I've been experiencing these terrible aches right here." She gestured toward her lower abdomen, her fingers brushing against the fabric of her blouse in a subtle tease.

"Let's take a look then," Emily replied, her pulse quickening at the sight of Samantha's deliberate touch.

"Oh, I should undress, shouldn't I?" Samantha suggested, her words dripping with a honeyed seductiveness that seemed out of place for the sterile environment.

"That won't be necessary for this type of examination," Emily countered, though her eyes betrayed her, lingering just a moment too long on the contour of Samantha's hips before she could catch herself.

"Of course, Doctor. But I want to make sure you can examine me thoroughly," Samantha insisted, her fingers deftly unbuttoning her blouse to reveal a hint of cleavage.

Emily swallowed hard. "Alright, if you think it'll help with the diagnosis," she conceded, turning away to give Samantha some semblance of privacy. Yet, the rustle of clothing behind her filled her mind with unprofessional thoughts.

"Is this better, Doctor?" Samantha asked, now stripped down to her bra and panties, standing vulnerable yet strangely powerful before Emily.

"Uh, yes, let's proceed," Emily said, forcing her gaze back to Samantha's face. She palpated Samantha's abdomen with clinical precision, searching for any sign of ailment, but found nothing amiss. "I can't seem to find anything wrong," she admitted, her brows knitting together in concentration.

"Maybe you're not looking in the right place," Samantha hinted, her blue eyes locked onto Emily's with an intensity that made the doctor's breath hitch.

"Where exactly do you feel the pain?" Emily asked, blushing.

"Right here," Samantha murmured, guiding Emily's hand lower, dangerously close to the elastic edge of her panties.

"Samantha, please," Emily stammered, attempting to retract her hand, but the heat emanating from Samantha's skin had already seared itself into her memory.

"Sorry, Doctor," Samantha teased with a coy smile, "But I thought you might want to investigate... thoroughly."

Emily's thoughts were a whirlwind of professional ethics clashing with raw desire. "I... We should..."

"Relax, Doctor," Samantha whispered, leaning in close enough for Emily to feel the warmth of her breath. "It's all part of the examination, isn't it?"

"I'm sorry, but I won't be able to help you here, you need ultrasound." Emily blushed, turning away.

"Ok, Dr. Parker, there's something I need to confess," Samantha said, shifting her position on the examination table, the paper crinkling beneath her. The vulnerability in her tone was meticulously crafted, a feigned nakedness that was as much a part of her arsenal as her physical allure.

Samantha was an experienced hunter and knew when to pull back a little.

"What is it, Samantha?" Emily stood by the examination table, her hands now safely tucked into the pockets of her white coat.

Samantha inhaled deeply, her chest rising and falling dramatically. "I lied about the pain. It's not... physical, not really." She paused, gauging Emily's reaction before continuing. "The truth is, I've never reached orgasm. Every time I get close, there's this overwhelming sensation that makes me pull back. It's like something is growing inside of me. Sorry for lying, I was too embarrassed."

Emily's eyes widened, both at the revelation and the unexpected connection she felt to it. The exactly same issue had haunted her own intimate moments, a barrier she'd never been able to overcome. "You're not alone in that," she admitted. Confessing such a personal struggle to a patient was uncharted territory for her.

"Really?" Samantha feigned surprise, though inwardly she rejoiced at the progress of her hunt. Emily's stepped right into Samantha's trap.

"Yes," Emily confirmed, her cheeks flushed with a mixture of embarrassment and relief. "It's actually why I became a doctor, to find a solution to... my issues. But I haven't found one yet. There were no cases like mine in literature until now."

"Perhaps we can find the solution together," Samantha suggested, her lips curling into an encouraging smile.

"Maybe," Emily replied.

"Thank you for trusting me with this," Samantha said softly, reaching out to gently touch Emily's arm. "Dr. Parker," Samantha continued, her voice a velvet caress that seemed to reach out and stroke Emily's professional resolve, "what if we looked at my... condition under medical observation? You could stimulate me and monitor my reactions, see what happens when I'm on the brink."

Emily hesitated, her mind warring between the tenets of medical professionalism and the undeniable pull of desire she felt toward this enigmatic woman before her. "I'm not sure that would be appropriate," she started, but was quickly interrupted.

"Emily," Samantha said with deliberate intimacy, "it's all in the name of science, isn't it? Observing natural responses for research purposes—there's nothing wrong with that. You said it yourself, up until now you were your only subject and it is impossible to be objective. Now you can look at the problem from the side and gain new insights that could help both of us."

The logic was sound, clinically detached and yet entirely seductive. Emily found herself nodding slowly, her heart pounding against her ribcage. She justified it as a necessary step, brushing aside the fact that the thought of bringing Samantha to climax stirred within her an arousal that was anything but scientific.

"Alright," Emily conceded, her voice betraying a hint of excitement she hadn't meant to show. "Purely for research, of course."

"Of course," Samantha echoed, a knowing gleam in her eye.

She couldn't wait to show Samantha her new cock.

As Emily's fingers began their careful stimulation, tracing the soft folds of Samantha's pussy with clinical precision, Samantha watched the doctor's face closely. The heat emanating from between Samantha's thighs was mirrored in the flush spreading across Emily's cheeks. It wasn't long before Samantha's subtle shifts and soft moans broke through Emily's professional facade.

"Emily..." Samantha breathed out, her voice husky with need as her hand reached up to pull Emily into a searing kiss.

The doctor's reservations melted away under the onslaught of passion. Their tongues danced together in a rhythm that echoed the growing intensity of their encounter. Emily's hand became bolder, more insistent, as she stroked Samantha's clit, eliciting gasps and whimpers that fueled her own burgeoning desire.

"Please," Samantha whispered against Emily's lips, her plea laced with unspoken promises.

Samantha's fingers dove under Emily's white coat and found her engorged clit.

Emily gasped, her body trembling as she pushed into Samantha's touch. Their actions were no longer professional, reasoned or detached. Unrestrained desire was weaving its intoxicating thread around them, pulling them both into a vortex of primal need and raw arousal.

Their bodies moved like well-oiled gears, seamlessly synchronizing with each other's rhythm as they polished each other's clits.

They were no longer doctor and patient; they were two women entwined in an intimate dance of pleasure and exploration. Samantha's fingers deftly found the sweet spot that made Emily shudder in delight.

"Doctor... Emily..." Samantha purred, her voice a symphony of desire that echoed Emily's own need. Her eyes sparkled with mischief and satisfaction as Emily whimpered under her skilled ministrations.

From there, their movements became more frantic, their breaths more labored. The sterile, clinical atmosphere of the examination room was replaced by an intoxicating mix of sweat and unbounded lust.

The moans that escaped their lips were not of pain but pleasure—a language so raw and primal it left no room for misunderstandings.

When the mounting pressure signaled Emily's impending release, Emily instinctively tried to withdraw, but Samantha's hands were swift, pinning Emily firmly, her grip a vice of determination.

"I have another confession to make," Samantha whispered, her eyes locking onto Emily's with fierce intensity. "I know the remedy for your condition. And I am about to show it to you."

Holding Emily firmly in place, Samantha stroked Emily's clit with religious zeal and Emily finally gave in to pleasure.

A tidal wave of sensation washed over Emily, making her gasp and buck against Samantha's touch. Her vision exploded into a myriad of colors, each one more vibrant than the last as the force of her orgasm rippled through her body. Emily's breath hitched in her throat, a strangled cry escaping her lips as she clung onto Samantha. It was a kind of ecstasy she had never experienced before – raw, unrestrained, and overwhelmingly intense.

As Emily tried to regain her sense of reality - her shaky fingers clutching onto Samantha's forearm like a lifeline - Samantha guided Emily's gaze downward.

Emily's breath hitched, her eyes widening in disbelief. There, burgeoning from her own body, was a sizable, throbbing cock—a manifestation both foreign and fucking huge and veiny and throbbing. Her shock was palpable, her mind racing to comprehend the physiological impossibility that now seemed an intrinsic part of her.

"What... How is this possible?" Emily stammered, her voice tinged with awe and confusion.

Samantha's face softened, her dominance giving way to triumph.

The hunt was a success.

Now was the time for the fun part.

"You're a futa, Emily. It's not just about having this," Samantha gestured at the impressive cock, "it's about discovering your true nature. You are a woman with a cock that is made for fucking."

Emily's emotions churned—a maelstrom of fear, excitement, and a dawning sense of liberation. She tentatively reached down, her fingers brushing against the velvety firmness of her new appendage. A jolt of pleasure surged through her, illuminating pathways of desire she had never imagined.

"But this is anatomically impossible! How do I have these new neural pathways, how the hell did this thing grew so quickly, there are no fucking stretch marks," Emily murmured, her scientific mind grappling with the implications. "I could win a Nobel Prize for this!"

"Before you revolutionize medicine," Samantha interjected, her tone laced with desire, "I need my prize." The seductive glint in Samantha's eye left no room for misunderstanding.

Their eyes locked, they let their fingertips roam over each other's bodies, tracing delicate lines on each other's skin.

Samantha's long, dark hair cascaded down her back, framing her exquisite face. Her piercing blue eyes were filled with desire, burning into Emily's very soul. Her full lips parted slightly, revealing a hint of her pearly teeth. The curve of her hips and the swell of her breasts enticed Emily, who found it increasingly difficult to resist touching her.

"God, you're so stunning," Emily breathed, her hands cupping Samantha's ample breasts.

"Look at you," Samantha purred, running her fingers down the smooth lines of Emily's sides. "You're like a goddess. A little futa goddess."

Emily closed her eyes, reveling in the sensation of Samantha's touch. She felt exposed and vulnerable, yet empowered and desired. Emily's short, curly red hair framed her warm brown eyes, magnifying their intensity.

"Touch me more, please," Emily whispered, biting her lower lip in anticipation.

"Of course, darling," Samantha replied, smirking confidently as she took control.

Samantha eagerly knelt before Emily, her gaze fixed on the throbbing cock between Emily's legs. Emily's eyes were wide with excitement as she gripped Samantha's hair, urging her forward.

"Go on," Emily hissed, her voice dripping with filth. "Let's try this thing out... for science."

Without hesitation, Samantha wrapped her luscious lips around Emily's pulsating cock, her lustful eyes never leaving the trembling doctor's face. The sensation was electric, sending shivers down Emily's spine as she gasped in pleasure.

"Fuck, that feels amazing," Emily moaned, her hands clutching at Samantha's hair. "Don't stop."

Samantha took Emily's cock deeper into her mouth, her tongue swirling around the sensitive head as she sucked voraciously. With her mouth filled with Emily's throbbing cock, she reached down to explore the doctor's wet pussy. Her fingers slid between the slick folds, feeling the heat and desire radiating from within. Emily's moans vibrated around her pulsating member, the sensation of Samantha's tongue and fingers sending her into a whirlwind of ecstasy.

"God, yes," Emily gasped, her hips bucking involuntarily as Samantha's fingers penetrated her. "Fuck, that feels so good!"

The unique experience of giving and receiving pleasure simultaneously overwhelmed Emily, her body quivering under Samantha's skillful touch. She couldn't help but scream out as waves of pleasure coursed through every inch of her being.

"More... please, more!" Emily pleaded, her eyes glazed over with lust.

Emily's mind raced as she tried to process the onslaught of sensations. Her thoughts were scattered, a cacophony of pleasure and need. All she could focus on was the warmth of Samantha's mouth around her cock and the delicious pressure of her fingers buried deep inside her pussy.

"Can't... take much more..." Emily panted, her body trembling.

"Then let's move to something even better," Samantha suggested as she withdrew her fingers and released Emily's cock from her mouth with an audible pop.

Samantha's hands gripped Emily's shoulders with surprising force, pushing her onto her back on the smooth examination table. Their bodies were flushed and radiating heat, causing the cool surface to feel even chillier against their skin. With a sense of urgency, Samantha climbed atop Emily, straddling her hips and locking eyes with the beautiful doctor. She guided the throbbing cock inside herself, feeling every inch as it filled her body with pleasure and desire.

"Ready for this?" Samantha asked with a wicked grin.

"Fuck me, Sam," Emily demanded, her voice hoarse with desire.

And so they began to thrust together, their bodies connecting with primal need as they fucked like dirty animals. Samantha's hips moved with practiced skill, riding Emily's cock with a fervor that left them both breathless.

As Samantha's sweet, juicy pussy gripped Emily's cock, her eyes rolled back in pleasure. She felt every inch of her member disappear between Samantha's folds, stretching and filling her. This new sensation was intense, both women gasping at the sensation of skin on skin. Samantha bounced on Emily's cock hard and fast, their hips meeting in a hypnotic rhythm that echoed throughout the normally sterile room.

"Oh god," Emily moaned, closing her eyes as pleasure coursed through her body. "Fuck, you feel so good." Her hands reached up to cup Samantha's plump ass, pulling her down for a deeper penetration.

Samantha leaned forward, letting their breasts touch as she began to grind against Emily's pelvis. Their bodies moved together in perfect synchronicity, the slap of skin on skin creating an intoxicating melody.

Emily's breath hitched as she looked up at Samantha's flushed face, her eyes fluttering shut from the pleasure coursing through her body. Her fingers dug into Samantha's hips, urging her to move faster and harder. The taste of Samantha on her tongue still lingered from their previous encounter, driving Emily wild with need.

"Your cock feels so fucking good inside me," Samantha panted, her nails digging into Emily's shoulders as she rode her hard and harder.

"Tell me how much you love it," Emily growled, her hands gripping Samantha's waist to pull her closer.

"Can't get enough of it," Samantha moaned. With a sultry smile, she added, "But now I want you to fuck me from behind."

Emily's eyes widened with eager anticipation, her breath quickening at the thought of what was to come. Samantha gracefully positioned herself on all fours on the examination table, the smooth curves of her back and buttocks arched enticingly. Emily couldn't resist the seductive display and moved in close, her hands gripping Samantha's hips firmly as she leaned in closer to explore every inch of her body.

"Are you ready?" Emily asked, her voice trembling with anticipation of fucking someone with her cock for the first time in her life.

"Give it to me," Samantha demanded, her blue eyes locked on Emily's.

With a deep breath, Emily plunged her throbbing cock into Samantha's wet pussy, eliciting a guttural moan from both women. The room filled with the sounds of their lustful union as Emily began pounding Samantha's tight cunt from behind. Emily was amazed at how natural it felt to move her hips this way, it felt as if fucking women was her second nature.

Her hands gripped Samantha's waist tighter as she pushed her throbbing cock deeper into her. Each thrust produced a chorus of gasps and moans that filled the room, matching the rhythm of their heaving bodies.

Samantha was a canvas of desire, alive under Emily's touch. Her whimpers and pleas went straight to Emily's core, creating an intoxicating mix of lust and power.

"Faster!" Samantha cried out, throwing a look over her shoulder that was equal parts challenge and pleading.

Emily smirked, the thrill of the chase igniting a spark in her as she resumed pounding Samantha with everything she had. She couldn't help but marvel at how tightly Samantha's pussy gripped her cock, each thrust evoking a mewl from the woman beneath her.

She moved one hand from Samantha's hip to grip her hair tightly. Guiding Samantha's head back to meet her gaze, their eyes locked in a shared intensity only heightened by their sweaty bodies' rhythmic dance.

"You're so fucking tight," Emily breathed into Samantha's ear, her voice raspy from exertion and lust.

"Your big fucking cock feels amazing, Em," Samantha panted, her body trembling with each powerful thrust.

"God, I can't get enough of fucking you," Emily groaned, reaching down to slap Samantha's round ass, leaving a stinging red mark.

"Fuck me harder, doctor," Samantha begged.

"Take my cock, you filthy slut," Emily growled, her nails digging into Samantha's flesh as she pounded her relentlessly.

Emily could feel her climax building, the pleasure becoming almost too much to bear. She pulled Samantha up by the hair, forcing her onto her feet while still impaled on Emily's rock-hard dick. Their bodies pressed together, sweat mingling as they looked deeply into each other's eyes.

"Kiss me, you horny bitch," Emily rasped, her hands roaming over Samantha's voluptuous form as their lips met in a passionate embrace.

Their tongues danced together, their moans mixing as they fucked standing up, the intensity of their lust threatening to consume them both. Samantha's fingers clawed at Emily's back, urging her on.

With a primal scream, Emily exploded inside Samantha, her first powerful ejaculation making her flesh explode. The feeling was divine, surreal, unlike anything she'd ever experienced before. She pumped Samantha full of her cum for the very first time in her life and it felt surreal.

The room still reverberated with the echoes of Emily's primal scream as her orgasm subsided. She stared into Samantha's eyes, mesmerized by the satisfaction she saw there.

"Em, I didn't come yet," Samantha panted, a wicked grin spreading across her face. "Get on your back. I need to ride that pretty face of yours."

Emily complied without hesitation, her eyes still wide with the exhilaration of her very first proper orgasm. Samantha straddled Emily's face, her dripping pussy hovering just above Emily's waiting mouth.

"Show me how much you worship my cunt, Dr. Parker," Samantha commanded.

"Like this?" Emily asked before eagerly pressing her lips against Samantha's soaked folds. Her tongue darted out, exploring every inch of Samantha's quivering sex. The taste of Samantha combined with her own cum that flowed out was intoxicating.

"Fuck, yes!" Samantha moaned, grinding her hips down onto Emily's face. "Don't stop!"

As Emily licked and sucked at Samantha's pussy, she couldn't help but reach for her own throbbing cock. Gripping it with both hands, she began to jerk herself off, the remnants of her previous release coating her fingers and smearing across her skin.

"Your pussy is so fucking delicious, Sam" Emily mumbled between licks, continuing to pleasure herself.

"Keep going, Em. I'm so close," Samantha gasped.

Emily slapped one of Samantha's bouncing breasts, her hand leaving an imprint on the sensitive flesh.

With a final shudder, Samantha succumbed to her climax, her body wracked with pleasure as she screamed Emily's name. As Samantha's orgasm washed over her, Emily continued to pump her own cock, desperate to experience another mind-shattering release.

"I see your cock is hungry for more?" Samantha asked with a mischievous grin, her voice thick with desire.

"Absolutely," Emily replied breathlessly as she gently pulled Samantha off of her and positioned her on her back upon the examination table. Their steamy gaze held each other's attention as they moved into the missionary position, Samantha's legs wrapping around Emily's waist, drawing her in even closer.

Emily's body trembled with excitement as she gazed at Samantha's slick, swollen pussy, still oozing with sperm. Her own throbbing cock ached for release as she positioned it at Samantha's entrance, feeling the warmth and wetness beckoning to her. With a primal growl, Emily thrust forward, burying herself within Samantha's tight walls and reveling in the sensation of their bodies joining together.

"Fuck, Emily! Your huge cock feels so good!" Samantha moaned, her fingers digging into Emily's shoulders.

As Emily picked up her pace, she could feel the intensity of their pleasure building. She leaned down to capture Samantha's lips in a passionate kiss, the taste of their combined arousal intoxicating.

Emily cried out, the feeling of being inside Samantha's pussy overwhelming her. The slap of skin on skin resonated through the room, echoing off the metal examination table and the walls. Her hips met Samantha's rhythmically, thrust for thrust, each one drawing a moan from her lover. The taste of their shared cum mixed with pussy juices and lingering desire as they kissed. Samantha's teeth nipped at Emily's lower lip, drawing blood as she ground against her.

Their bodies moved together, each thrust becoming more powerful than the next. Emily felt possessed by this newfound lust, as if it had always been a part of her. She slapped Samantha's breasts in time with her movements, sending a jolt of pleasure through her body. Samantha gripped Emily's hair tightly, guiding their kisses as they moved in perfect sync.

"You feel so fucking good," Emily panted between breaths while she fucked Samantha harder. "Your pussy is so hot and wet."

Samantha groaned in agreement, arching her back to meet each thrust. "I could get used to this," she gasped out between gasps for air. Her nails dug into Emily's shoulders, leaving half-moons of red in the skin beneath. "So fucking good..."

"Sam, I'm gonna make you cum so hard," Emily panted between thrusts, her hips slamming against Samantha's as she drove her cock deeper and harder into her lover. "You ready for it?"

"God, yes! Destroy my little pussy with that big, thick cock of yours! You owe me that!" Samantha cried out, her eyes rolling back in ecstasy.

Emily's determination only grew stronger, fueled by the lustful cries of Samantha. Her entire focus was on giving Samantha the most intense orgasm she had ever experienced.

"Em... Em, I'm so close! Oh, fuck, don't stop!" Samantha screamed, her body quivering on the brink of release.

"Come with me, Sam" Emily urged, feeling her own climax rapidly approaching.

And with one final, powerful thrust, they both exploded into orgasm, their cries of pleasure mingling as they clung to each other, riding the waves of ecstasy that washed over them.

Their bodies shuddered together in unison, caught in the powerful throes of their climax. Emily could feel her cum gushing out and filling Samantha, seeping out to coat their conjoined bodies. Samantha's internal muscles clamped around Emily's cock, milking her for everything she had. The sensation was mind-shattering, forcing a cry of pleasure from Emily's lips that echoed loudly in the room.

Samantha shivered beneath her, mouth slack as low moans of pleasure fell from her lips. Her eyes were closed tightly, lost in the ecstasy surging through her. A sheen of sweat covered their bodies, adding to the heat that radiated off them.

Finally, after what felt like hours, their bodies began to untense and relax into the more manageable aftershocks of orgasm. Emily gently pulled out of Samantha, a small whimper escaping Samantha's lips at the loss. She collapsed next to her on the table, both breathing heavily in exertion.

Emily reached out to intertwine their hands, a soft smile on her face when Samantha squeezed back.

As they lay on the examination table, panting and spent, Emily couldn't help but ponder her newfound anatomy. "You know, I'm not sure if I should be examining this more or just using it to fuck everything that moves," she mused aloud, a playful smile tugging at her lips.

Samantha laughed, her blue eyes sparkling with mischief. "Well, Em, I think you can probably guess my answer to that."

"True," Emily chuckled. "Hey, are you free for another 'examination' tomorrow?"

"Sorry, Doctor," Samantha replied, running her fingers through Emily's damp curls. "I've got a business meeting tomorrow."

The End.

Futa Hunter: Bossy Manager

Samantha Carter strode into the gleaming lobby of Lewis Marketing with the poise of a panther on the prowl. She was an embodiment of allure, her long, dark hair cascading like a sable waterfall over the shoulders of her tailored navy blazer, which hugged her curves in just the right way to suggest without overtly revealing. Her skirt was a balancing act of professionalism and seduction—short enough to captivate but long enough to maintain decorum. Samantha's piercing blue eyes scanned the environment, looking for her prey.

The office exuded a modern, minimalist charm, the walls adorned with abstract art that commanded attention while sleek furniture offered a welcome devoid of clutter. The air hummed with the energy of ambition and success, a fitting stage for the owner, Sophia Lewis.

Sophia sat behind a large mahogany desk, her posture not merely upright but commanding, as if the chair was a throne she was born to occupy. With sleek black hair that framed her face and those same arresting blue eyes as Samantha, there was an electric mirroring between the two women. Her attire—a crisp white blouse paired with a form-fitting pencil skirt—spoke of a woman who wielded power with the same ease as elegance.

It was her, Samantha's target.

"Miss Carter, I presume?" Sophia's voice cut through the space with practiced authority.

"Indeed," Samantha replied, allowing a small smile to play upon her lips as she extended a hand. "Thank you for seeing me today."

"Please, have a seat." Sophia gestured to the chair opposite her desk, her fingers brushing Samantha's in a fleeting exchange that sent a spark of anticipation down Samantha's spine.

Samantha was a professional futa hunter, but each time she met a new uninitiated futa it felt like the very first time and that's why Samantha was a futa hunter.

As Samantha settled into the chair, she caught Sophia's gaze, holding it with an intensity that bordered on daring. "Your reputation precedes you, Miss Lewis. Your company is renowned for its cutting-edge campaigns and impressive clientele roster."

"Flattery won't help you get this job, Miss Carter," Sophia quipped, though her eyes shimmered with curiosity.

"Only stating facts," Samantha countered smoothly. "But let's talk about what I can bring to the table."

"Please, do enlighten me."

"My experience with international markets is extensive," Samantha began, crossing her legs and noting the brief flicker of Sophia's eyes downward. "I've spearheaded campaigns that resulted in a thirty percent increase in global sales for our clients."

"Interesting," Sophia murmured, leaning forward. "And your approach to new media?"

"Aggressive and forward-thinking," Samantha asserted. "For instance, leveraging influencer partnerships has yielded a significant uptick in engagement rates. Combine that with data-driven strategies, and we can deliver not just content but conversion."

"Conversion," Sophia repeated, musing on the word as if tasting it. "I like that."

Samantha smiled, a slow, deliberate curve of her lips. "I thought you might. It's all about transforming potential into reality, wouldn't you agree?"

"Transformation," Sophia echoed, a glint of something more than professional interest in her gaze. "Yes, I would very much agree."

Samantha smirked. Sophia had no idea about the transformation that awaited her oh so very soon.

Their conversation continued, a dance of words and glances that wove a web of implicit understanding. Samantha navigated the interview with the confidence of one who knew their value, her flirtatious undertones never detracting from the solid foundation of her expertise.

"Your portfolio is impressive," Sophia admitted, tapping a manicured finger on a resume that seemed woefully inadequate to capture Samantha's essence. "You have a knack for turning challenges into triumphs."

"Challenges excite me," Samantha said, her tone laced with double entendre. "I find the thrill of the hunt... invigorating."

"Is that so?" Sophia's eyebrow arched, a silent challenge of its own.

"Absolutely," Samantha assured, her eyes locked onto Sophia's. "It's about chasing down every opportunity and seizing it with both hands."

"Indeed," Sophia breathed out.

"Shall we discuss how I might seize the opportunities here at Lewis Marketing?" Samantha asked, tilting her head slightly, inviting Sophia into her game.

"Let's," Sophia agreed, her voice a velvet caress.

Even as the interview progressed, Samantha remained acutely aware of the tension simmering beneath the surface, a magnetic pull drawing them towards a collision course with destiny. This was no ordinary job interview, and Samantha Carter was no ordinary applicant. She was a hunter—and her prey was finally within reach.

Sophia leaned forward, her gaze piercing as she posed another complex marketing strategy question, her dominance in the professional arena undeniably alluring to Samantha. "And how would you navigate a market downturn with an aggressive campaign?"

Without breaking eye contact, Samantha laid out a detailed plan involving risk assessment and innovative branding techniques. As she spoke, Sophia's fingers brushed against Samantha's hand, ostensibly in the process of handing over her resume.

"Unexpected challenges are where true innovation shines," Samantha concluded, allowing her own fingers to linger a moment longer than necessary against Sophia's.

"Very insightful," Sophia murmured, the corner of her mouth lifting in a half-smile. She leaned back in her chair, appraising Samantha with a look that spoke volumes.

"Ms. Carter," Sophia began, her voice smooth as silk, "you've handled every curveball I've thrown your way with impressive finesse. You're clearly adept at playing... complex games."

"Only the most stimulating ones," Samantha countered.

"Then you'll be pleased to know you've just secured yourself a position here." Sophia's words were deliberate, each syllable a tender stroke against Samantha's ambition.

"Thank you, Ms. Lewis," Samantha replied, her voice steady despite the rush of victory surging through her. "I'm eager to prove myself and contribute to the team."

"Call me Sophia," the businesswoman instructed, her tone inviting a more intimate rapport. "And something tells me you'll fit right in."

Samantha stood, extending her hand, which Sophia grasped firmly—a symbolic sealing of their burgeoning partnership. "I look forward to it, Sophia."

"Welcome to Lewis Marketing, Samantha," Sophia said, standing as well to maintain the equality between them. "I have a feeling you're going to make quite the impact."

"Count on it," Samantha assured her with a knowing smile. The hunt had truly begun.

***

Samantha was the first to arrive at the office, eager to prove herself. She dove into her work, finishing task after task with laser focus. Nothing could distract her.

When Sophia emerged from her office, Samantha's heart skipped a beat. She watched as Sophia strode through the office, her tight skirt accentuating the sway of her hips. Their eyes met for a brief moment, and a sly smile curled Sophia's lips. Heat flooded Samantha's cheeks as she looked away, her cunt throbbing with need.

She was so close she could feel it.

As the workday progressed, Samantha completed her assignments ahead of schedule. She offered to help her coworkers, encouraging them to work more efficiently. Though she didn't interact with her boss directly, she could feel the weight of her gaze, judging her every move.

By the time the office had emptied, Samantha was trembling with equal parts anticipation and dread. She had impressed Sophia with her work ethic, but would it be enough?

Sophia emerged from her office again, the click of her heels echoing through the empty space. Samantha looked up as Sophia stopped in front of her desk, hands on her hips.

"Well done, Samantha," Sophia purred. "You've exceeded my expectations."

Samantha swallowed hard, anticipating the final phase of the hunt. "Thank you, Sophia."

Sophia leaned down, bracing her hands on the edge of the desk. Her blouse gaped open, and Samantha glimpsed the swell of her breasts. She bit her lip, unable to look away.

"I think you deserve a reward," Sophia continued, her voice dropping to a sultry whisper. "Don't you agree?"

Samantha nodded, her mouth dry. She would get her reward, but Sophia had no idea what what's coming.

Sophia smiled, slow and predatory. "Good girl."

She took Samantha's chin in her hand, tilting her head up to meet her gaze. Samantha shuddered, drowning in the depths of Sophia's eyes.

"Now, let's discuss how you'll be repaying my generosity..."

Samantha's heart raced as Sophia traced a fingertip down her throat. She swallowed hard, arousal pooling between her legs.

"I was thinking a massage might help relieve some of my tension," Sophia purred. She arched a brow. "If you're interested, that is."

"Yes," Samantha breathed. She cleared her throat, trying to compose herself. "I would be happy to provide you a massage, Sophia."

Sophia's smile widened. "Obedient. Wonderful. Follow me, then."

She sashayed toward her office, hips swaying. Samantha scrambled to follow, anticipation building with each step.

Once inside, Sophia locked the door behind them. She turned to Samantha, eyes dark with desire.

"Well? Get to work."

Samantha guided Sophia to the plush sofa along the wall, helping her settle onto her stomach. She straddled Sophia's thighs, hands sliding up her back.

"Just relax," Samantha murmured. She kneaded the tense muscles of Sophia's shoulders, eliciting a soft groan.

Emboldened, she worked her way down Sophia's back, massaging each knot and ache. Sophia squirmed beneath her, hips grinding into the sofa. Samantha bit her lip, the ache between her own legs becoming nearly unbearable.

She slid her hands along Sophia's sides, inching upward. Her thumbs brushed the sides of Sophia's breasts and Sophia turned under Samantha, lying on her back.

Sophia gasped, arching into the touch. "Don't tease me, girl."

"Yes, Sophia," Samantha breathed. She slid her hands over Sophia's breasts, squeezing and massaging the soft flesh.

Sophia moaned, the sound shooting straight to Samantha's core. "That's it," she purred, rolling her hips. "Take your reward."

Samantha shuddered, desire burning in her veins like molten fire.

Samantha slid her hands down Sophia's torso, fingers hooking into the waistband of her skirt. She tugged it down over Sophia's hips, leaving her bare from the waist down.

Sophia spread her legs, giving Samantha full access. Samantha licked her lips at the sight of Sophia's glistening pussy, already wet and ready for her touch.

Soon, so very soon there will be a nice cock hanging there.

She slid two fingers through Sophia's folds, circling her clit. Sophia bucked against her hand with a desperate moan.

"Please, Samantha," she begged. "I need —"

Samantha thrust two fingers into Sophia's cunt, curling them against her front wall. Sophia cried out, inner walls clenching around Samantha's fingers.

"That's it," Samantha crooned, setting a brutal pace. She leaned down, taking one of Sophia's nipples between her teeth and biting down.

Suddenly, Sophia pushed Samantha back. "Ok, that's enough, time for me to pleasure you."

Samantha grinned. This was it, the killing blow.

With expert precision, she pinned Sophia to the sofa. "You never had an orgasm before, didn't you? Every time you get close, you sense something awakening within you and pull back. This is why you are such a success, pouring all that sexual frustration into your work. Not anymore."

Before Sophia could react Samantha began fingerblasting Sophia's pussy like there was no tomorrow.

Sophia screamed, back arching off the floor as her very first orgasm crashed over her in waves. Her cunt clenched rhythmically around Samantha's fingers, hot wetness gushing over her hand.

Samantha gentled her touch, working Sophia through the aftershocks. A strange pulsing sensation filled the air, almost like a heartbeat.

Sophia's body jerked, a shocked gasp leaving her lips. Samantha glanced down — and froze.

A massive cock was emerging from between Sophia's legs, red and swollen and dripping precum. It grew larger and larger, finally stopping at what must have been ten inches long and thick enough to stretch Sophia's cunt wide.

Samantha stared, mouth watering. Her futa hunter instincts roared to life, primal desire flooding her senses.

"W-what's happening?" Sophia asked, panic edging into her tone. She tried to sit up, but the new weight between her legs threw off her balance.

"Shh, relax," Samantha soothed. She ran a hand up the length of Sophia's cock, squeezing gently. Sophia whimpered, hips jerking into the touch.

"You're becoming a futa," Samantha explained. "Your true nature is awakening at last." She stroked Sophia again, twisting her wrist. "And what a glorious awakening it is."

Sophia swallowed hard, eyes fluttering shut. "I don't understand," she said weakly. "What does this mean?"

"It means you were made to fuck," Samantha purred, "and be fucked. Your cock will bring you pleasure beyond your wildest dreams — and now, you have the power to do the same for others."

She leaned down, running her tongue along the head of Sophia's cock. Sophia cried out, hands flying to grip Samantha's hair.

"Please," Sophia begged, trembling. "Show me. I need —"

"I know exactly what you need." Samantha wrapped her fingers around Sophia's massive dick. "It's time for your first futa fucking. And my real prize."

"Open your mouth, Samantha," Sophia commanded, her voice a silken thread laced with iron. "I want to see those lips wrapped around my cock."

Samantha obeyed without hesitation, parting her full lips as Sophia stepped forward. The sight of Samantha's warm, wet mouth eagerly awaiting her made Sophia's newly discovered appendage throb with need. She guided herself into the welcoming cavern, suppressing a moan at the first touch of Samantha's tongue swirling around the head of her cock.

"Fuck, that's it," Sophia breathed out. "Use that gorgeous mouth of yours, make me feel good."

Samantha hummed in affirmation, the vibrations sending jolts of pleasure coursing through Sophia. Her hands found their way into Samantha's hair, guiding the rhythm with gentle tugs.

The sensation was unlike anything Sophia had ever experienced; the pressure, the heat, the slickness—it was all intoxicating. Her mind spun with the realization that this powerful feeling between her legs was no longer just a fantasy.

And the weirdest thing of all is that it felt so natural, like she was born with it.

Samantha slurped and sucked, taking more of Sophia's shaft into her mouth with each thrust. Her cheeks hollowed as she bobbed back and forth, eyes watering as Sophia's cock nudged the back of her throat.

"Your mouth is fucking perfect for sucking cock, Samantha," Sophia praised.

Samantha gazed up at Sophia through teary lashes, her eyes pleading for more. She could taste the salty pre-cum leaking from Sophia's tip.

But the pleasure was only one facet of her growing desire. Sophia wanted more—she needed to see Samantha unravel beneath her, she needed to see what her new cock was truly capable of. With a gentle but firm pull, she guided Samantha off her cock.

"Stand up," Sophia instructed, watching as Samantha rose gracefully to her feet. The predatory gleam in Samantha's eyes did nothing to diminish Sophia's assertive demeanor.

"Such a beautiful body," Sophia murmured, her hands tracing the curves of Samantha's form as she began to undress her. Fabric whispered against skin, revealing the prize beneath: Samantha's perky breasts, her flat stomach, the soft mound between her thighs that promised untold delights.

"Good thing I hired you," Sophia said, her fingers skimming over Samantha's exposed flesh.

"Actually," Samantha replied with a coy smile, stepping closer, "it was I who hunted you. This is what I do, I hunt uninitiated futas and awaken them." Her voice was a purr, a soft vibration that resonated with the tension in the room.

Their lips met in a searing kiss, tongues tangling in a dance as old as time. Hands roved with purpose, squeezing flesh and eliciting gasps from both women.

"Your cunt is going to feel so good wrapped around my dick," Sophia whispered against Samantha's lips. "Now present your ass to me."

Samantha obliged, turning around and bending over the side of the couch, her round, perfectly sculpted ass presented in delicious offering. She shivered with anticipation as Sophia stepped behind her, one hand gripping her new found cock, the other trailing lightly down Samantha's backside.

"Such a perfect ass," Sophia mused aloud, eyes rapturous at the carnal sight before her. She gave Samantha's ass a gentle slap, smirking at the startled gasp that echoed through the room. Goosebumps erupted along her skin and her nipples hardened into taut peaks.

Sophia's hands gripped Samantha's hips, her fingers digging into soft flesh with ownership as she lined herself up.

"Ready for me?" Sophia growled low in Samantha's ear.

"Fuck yes," Samantha breathed out, arching her back to present herself even more invitingly.

With a firm thrust, Sophia entered her from behind, eliciting a sharp cry that echoed off the glass panes of the office. Sophia gasped at the sensation of being inside Samantha, the warmth and tightness enveloping her cock felt almost too much to bear.

Sophia held her waist, steadying her as she started to move, slow and measured at first. The sensation was addictive; the pressure of

Sophia inside her, the heat seeping through her body and pooling down to the core of her lust.

With every thrust, Sophia stretched Samantha wider, reaching deeper into the place that no one else ever had. Samantha's breath hitched each time, a shudder running through her in delight.

The rhythm quickened as Sophia let go of any remaining control. Determined grunts accompanied each drive while Samantha moaned unabashedly at the intensity of it all. Her hands fisted into the fabric of the couch beneath them, gripping tight to keep herself grounded amid waves of pleasure that threatened to wash everything else away.

Sophia reveled in every whimper and cry that slipped from Samantha's lips - they were proof of her strength, her dominance – and it only made the arousal coursing through her veins all the more potent.

Now the rhythm was relentless, the sound of skin slapping against skin a decadent symphony. Sophia's hand left red marks on Samantha's ass, each slap punctuating the air with a promise of deeper pleasures.

"Such a perfect, tight little ass," Sophia praised. "Made for being fucked hard."

"Harder," Samantha demanded, pushing back against Sophia's cock with equal fervor. She reveled in the control she had relinquished, allowing Sophia to dominate her body.

Sophia complied, driving into Samantha with increased fervor. Each thrust sent waves of pleasure crashing through them both, and Samantha's moans became a mantra urging Sophia on.

"Your pussy... it's fucking divine," Sophia snarled, her nails scoring Samantha's thighs as she pulled her closer, seeking even deeper penetration.

"Show me what you've got, boss," Samantha challenged, her blue eyes flashing in the dim light.

"Get on top," Sophia commanded, breathless with arousal as they shifted positions. "Ride me."

She didn't waste any time. She straddled Sophia's thighs, aligning herself with Sophia's erect cock. Then slowly, torturously slow, she sank down onto it, her breasts bouncing enticingly. Sophia's hands found those full mounds, squeezing roughly in time with Samantha's movements.

"Look at these tits," Sophia said, her thumbs flicking over hardened nipples. "So fucking beautiful when they bounce."

Samantha grinned as she rode Sophia harder. She leaned forward, her hair cascading around them like a dark veil, to capture Sophia's lips in a searing kiss.

With a gasp, Sophia broke the kiss, her lips swollen and parted as she let out a string of dirty praises. Her mind was consumed with the sensation of her cock being enveloped by the warm, wet walls of Samantha's cunt. The sight of Samantha riding her, her hips undulating against Sophia's body, was almost too much to bear. Sophia's hands roamed over Samantha's toned figure, feeling the firmness and smoothness of her skin as she rode her with urgency. It was a sensory overload that threatened to push Sophia over the edge, her breath coming in quick pants as she surrendered herself to the intense pleasure coursing through every inch of her body.

"Fuck, keep going, just like that," Sophia urged, her hips bucking up to meet Samantha's descent.

"Only if you admit it," Samantha taunted, slowing her pace teasingly. "Admit that you love this cock."

"I fucking love it," Sophia confessed, her words torn from her in a ragged breath. "Best decision I ever made, hiring a futa hunter like you."

"Then come for me," Samantha whispered, her blue eyes locked onto Sophia's. "Show me how much you love it."

Gleaming with a sheen of exertion, Samantha slid from the saddle of Sophia's hips. She knelt before Sophia, her eyes glinting with purpose, and took Sophia's erect cock into her hands with the expertise of one who relished the hunt and the prize. Her tongue traced the length of Sophia's shaft slowly, provocatively, before she wrapped her lips around it.

"Like this?" Samantha murmured against Sophia's skin, her voice a velvet caress as she looked up through her thick lashes.

"Fuck... Yes," Sophia groaned, her fingers threading through Samantha's dark hair to guide her movements. Each suck, each flick of that talented tongue unraveled her completely.

Samantha's mouth was a warm haven, an enveloping wetness that pulsed with every heartbeat. The sensation of fullness, the suction—it was unlike anything Sophia had ever felt. As Samantha's head bobbed, taking her deeper, Sophia's legs trembled, her world narrowing to the hot cavern of Samantha's mouth.

"God, your mouth is heaven," Sophia panted, her hips twitching involuntarily. "I'm close."

"Fill my mouth with your cum."

These words tipped Sophia over, and she erupted. Her orgasm was a divine cataclysm, stars bursting behind her eyelids as her cock spasmed. The first spurt filled Samantha's mouth, followed by another, and another, until the warmth of her release bathed Samantha's tongue. It was euphoria manifest—the pulsing release, the sense of emptiness turned satisfaction, the throbbing pleasure that left her gasping for air.

"Fuck, I've never..." Sophia's voice trailed off into soft moans as she watched Samantha swallow, savoring her essence like it was the finest ambrosia. "That was..."

"Divine?" Samantha finished for her, her lips glossed with the remnants of Sophia's pleasure. "I know. I live for this."

Sophia, still reeling from the aftershocks, nodded, her chest heaving. "I didn't realize how good... How could I never have known?"

"Because you needed someone to show you," Samantha said with a smirk. "And you should know, futas don't need to stop after just one."

"Really?" Sophia raised an eyebrow.

"Absolutely," Samantha affirmed, standing to her feet. She leaned back on the office table, the cold surface a stark contrast to the heat of their bodies. "See your dick is still hard. Come fuck me again, no waiting necessary."

"Damn," Sophia breathed out, her strength returning as if on command. Gently, Sophia lifted Samantha onto the table. With careful precision, she parted Samantha's thighs, revealing the glistening warmth of her innermost desires. The slick wetness of Samantha's pussy enveloped Sophia's cock with an eager embrace as she entered her once more.

"More," Samantha hissed, locking her legs around Sophia's waist. "Harder."

Sophia complied, setting a fast and intense pace, each thrust punctuated by the slap of flesh against flesh. Her mind was alight with lust and power, the incredible revelation of her stamina coursing through her like wildfire.

"Your cunt feels so fucking good," Sophia growled, her gaze locked on where their bodies joined. "So tight, so perfect for my dick."

Sweat dripped down Sophia's forehead, but she didn't slow, didn't falter—she only drove harder, chasing the blissful high that Samantha promised lay just within reach.

The office was filled with the carnal sounds of their bodies slapping together, a relentless rhythm that had both women spiraling toward a peak neither had scaled before.

"Fuck, Samantha," Sophia panted, her voice thick with desire and exertion as she drove into the velvety grip of Samantha's cunt. "I'm going to come so hard inside you."

"Then do it," Samantha challenged again. "Show me what you've got, boss lady. Fill me up."

Sophia felt every ridge of Samantha's tight channel clenching around her cock, drawing her inexorably towards release.

"Your pussy is divine," Sophia groaned, feeling the tight coil of impending orgasm winding tighter within her core. "Designed for my cock."

"Yesss..." Samantha arched her back, her nails scoring Sophia's skin.

The words were barely out when their bodies convulsed in unison, a cataclysmic orgasm ripping through them. Sophia's vision whited out as she flooded Samantha's depths, her cock throbbing with the most potent release she'd ever experienced. Samantha's own climax echoed Sophia's, her walls milking every drop from the pulsating member buried deep inside her.

They collapsed in a tangle of limbs, chests heaving as they basked in the afterglow. Sophia's mind reeled, her thoughts a swirl of satisfaction and disbelief. She pressed her forehead against Samantha's shoulder, their sweat mingling as they caught their breaths.

"Every girl in the office deserves a reward for their hard work," Sophia murmured, tracing circles on Samantha's flushed skin. "I'll have to fuck each one just like this... but first, I want you again tomorrow."

"Tomorrow?" Samantha's chuckle was airy, spent. "I think I'll take some time off work."

The End.

Futa Hunter: Sensual Bartender

The chill of the evening air clung to Samantha's skin as she sauntered down the dimly lit street, her heels clicking a lonely rhythm against the pavement. Her reflection in the shop windows betrayed the smolder of mild depression that clouded her usually sparkling blue eyes—a lustful malaise born of unquenched desires and an itch for a connection that only a certain kind could satisfy.

A futa hunter by nature, Samantha's prowess lay in awakening those who harbored latent gifts, but lately she couldn't find any. With no uninitiated futas crossing her path, she probably would have to let an ordinary man pick her up.

Pushing open the door of the first bar that beckoned her wandering steps, Samantha slid onto a stool with the ease of a shadow merging into darkness. The place hummed with the low murmur of patrons lost in their own worlds of booze and banter, but it was the bartender who ensnared Samantha's attention like a siren's call.

"Evening. What can I get you?" she asked, her voice a smooth pour of whiskey over ice that sent a shiver down Samantha's spine.

Her instincts kicked in, years of experience screaming at her to take a closer look at the bartender.

"Surprise me," Samantha replied, her gaze flickering over the bartender's form. There was something about the way she moved—graceful yet restrained—as if her body held secrets begging to be whispered into the night. "I'm Samantha, by the way."

"Jasmine," the bartender returned with a tentative smile, her deep brown eyes meeting Samantha's with an unknowing innocence.

"Nice to meet you, Jasmine," Samantha purred, accepting the drink slid her way. She took a sip, the liquid heat fueling her intuition. "You're quite the enigma, aren't you?"

"Am I?" Jasmine's question came out more like a challenge, laced with a shyness that only confirmed Samantha's suspicions. Futa nature, restricted by fear of the unknown.

"Definitely," Samantha said, leaning forward to close the gap between them. "There's a depth to you... Something extraordinary beneath the surface."

Jasmine flushed, tucking a curly lock behind her ear. "You think so?"

"Absolutely," Samantha affirmed, her voice dropping to a whisper. "I have a knack for sensing...hidden potential."

Jasmine smiled and quickly turned away to wipe a perfectly clean glass.

Samantha's heart quickened, her predatory instincts sharpening as she observed Jasmine's body language—the subtle shift of weight from one foot to the other, the nervous bite of her full lip. It was like watching a butterfly poised on the brink of unfurling its wings.

"Tell me, Jasmine," Samantha ventured, her tone silk-wrapped steel, "have you ever felt like there's something inside you, just waiting to break free?"

"Sometimes," Jasmine admitted, the confession spilling out amidst the clinking glasses and the hum of conversation that filled the bar around them. "But I don't really know what it is."

"Maybe I can help you figure it out," Samantha offered, a knowing smile playing on her lips as she took another sip, her mind alight with the thrill of the chase.

"Maybe you can," Jasmine murmured, her guarded reserve melting into curiosity under Samantha's intense gaze.

It was the dance Samantha knew all too well—a rhythm of seduction and revelation, each step drawing them closer to the edge where ecstasy and identity blurred into one. She had found her prey, and the night was ripe with promise.

"Stick around after your shift," Samantha suggested, her voice a velvet caress. "I'll show you a world you've never dreamed of."

"Okay," Jasmine breathed out, the word barely audible over the pulsing beat of the bar, but loud enough for Samantha's eager ears.

Tonight, the hunt was on, and Samantha Carter felt alive with the anticipation of awakening yet another beautiful creature to their truest self.

"Looks like you've already got a fan club," a voice slurred from behind Samantha, thick with alcohol and entitlement. She turned to find a man leering at her, his eyes greedily taking in her form. "How about we get out of here and I show you a real good time?" The man looked pathetic, posing a pitiful contrast to the subtle beauty she was about to unfold in Jasmine.

He was tall and lanky, with greasy hair slicked back and a thick, unkempt beard. He was dressed in a mismatched suit, the colors clashing against each other. He reeked of alcohol and stale cigarettes, his breath heavy and sour. The stench intensified as he moved closer, making Samantha want to gag.

"That's very kind of you," Samantha said, her tone chillingly polite as those ice blue eyes landed on him. "But I'm already committed for the evening." She gestured vaguely towards the counter where Jasmine busied herself with other customers, avoiding their gaze.

The man's face twisted into a scowl at her rejection. "What are you on about, just let me buy you a drink."

Samantha's blue eyes frosted over. "Told you, I'm not interested," she said firmly, hoping to quash his advances without causing a scene.

"Come on, don't be like that," he persisted, stepping closer.

"Back off," Samantha warned, her voice dropping an octave.

"Fine, stuck up bitch," the man spat, swaying slightly as his gaze landed on Jasmine. "What about you, sweetheart? You look like you could use some fun."

"Leave her alone," Samantha interjected sharply, standing protectively in front of Jasmine.

"Or what?" the man sneered, squaring up to Samantha as if he relished the challenge.

"Or you'll find out exactly why it would've been smarter to crawl back into whatever hole you oozed out from," Samantha shot back, her patience worn thin. Her muscles tensed, ready to spring into action should words fail to deter him.

"Whatever," he grumbled, finally turning away, realizing perhaps that this prey had teeth. He stumbled off, leaving the air charged and Jasmine visibly shaken.

"Are you okay?" Samantha asked, her tone softening as she turned to Jasmine, whose eyes were wide with a mixture of fear and gratitude.

"Yes, thanks to you," Jasmine replied, her voice trembling slightly. "I... I don't know how to thank you."

"Thank me after your shift," Samantha suggested with a gentle firmness. "We have much to discuss, you and I."

Jasmine managed a small, nervous smile before turning back to her duties behind the bar. Samantha settled herself in a corner where she could keep an eye on things. Every now and then, their eyes met, and Samantha would offer a reassuring nod, making Jasmine blush and quickly look away.

Samantha felt the anticipation building within her as she waited, sipping at her drink slowly, feeling the weight of the night's promise heavy in her belly. She watched the minutes tick by until finally, the last call was announced, and the remaining patrons began to stagger out into the dark streets.

Samantha took her place outside the bar, leaning against the wall in the shadows. The cool night air did little to quell the heat that pulsed through her veins. Her thoughts were a mix of predatory excitement and calculated patience; she knew how to wait for her prey.

As the lights inside the establishment dimmed, signaling its closure, Jasmine emerged, flipping the sign to 'Closed' with an exhausted sigh. Her relief at the end of her shift was palpable even from a distance.

"Hey!" a slurred voice called out from the darkness, and both women stiffened. It was the asshole from earlier, apparently on the hunt of his own.

Too bad for him, because Samantha was a way superior hunter.

"Hey, pretty thing, you owe me some company," he slurred, stumbling toward Jasmine, who backed away instinctively.

"Back off," Samantha's voice cut through the night, icy and sharp. She stepped forward, placing herself between Jasmine and the man with an unyielding stance.

"Ah, the cockblocker returns," the man sneered.

"Last warning," Samantha said, her eyes narrowing into dangerous slits. She was coiled tight, every muscle ready to defend her prey from the vulture.

"Fine! You bitches deserve each other," the man spat, throwing his hands up in defeat. He stumbled backward, mumbling curses under his breath as he disappeared into the darkness.

"Thank you," Jasmine breathed out, her body visibly relaxing as the threat receded. "I don't know what I would've done if you hadn't been here."

"Let's get you home, Jasmine," Samantha suggested, her voice low and soothing. "You're safe now."

"Okay," Jasmine agreed. As they walked, Samantha felt that tonight was going to be a revelation for them both.

"Would you... like to come up?" Jasmine's voice was tentative but laced with a newfound warmth as they reached the entrance of her modest apartment building.

"Thought you'd never ask," Samantha replied, her lips curving into a smile.

They ascended the stairs, their footsteps echoing in the quiet corridor. With every step, Samantha could feel the palpable excitement mingling with nervous anticipation emanating from Jasmine.

"Here we are," Jasmine said, unlocking her door and ushering Samantha inside. The apartment was cozy, with soft lighting and a personal touch that made it inviting. It seemed to reflect Jasmine's shy personality, with its muted colors and understated elegance. Samantha took a moment to breathe in the scent of Jasmine's home, a mix of vanilla and something uniquely Jasmine.

"So, this is my humble abode," Jasmine's voice wavered slightly as she stepped aside to let Samantha take in the space.

"It's lovely," Samantha replied sincerely. She took a step further into the apartment, her eyes casually scanning the room before they landed back on Jasmine. "And it suits you."

Jasmine blushed at the comment but didn't avert her gaze. Samantha could see the curiosity welling up within her, mirroring her own desire to delve deeper into their connection. It was like watching a blossom slowly unfurl under the warm caress of the sun.

"Thanks," Jasmine finally replied, a blush creeping up her neck. "Can I get you something to drink? Or..."

"Or?" Samantha echoed, closing the distance between them. Her voice dropped to a husky whisper. "How about you show me where you unwind after a long night?"

"Sure," Jasmine said, her earlier shyness dissipating as she led Samantha by the hand to the bedroom. It was a sanctuary of soft fabrics and muted colors.

"Relax," Samantha murmured, turning Jasmine to face her. "I've got you."

Their eyes locked, and in that moment, the world outside ceased to exist.

"Sam..." Jasmine breathed out.

"Shh," Samantha hushed her gently, leaning in to capture Jasmine's lips with her own. The kiss was slow, exploratory at first, but it quickly deepened as Jasmine responded with equal fervor.

Samantha's hands roamed over Jasmine's body, tracing the outline of her curves through her clothing before deftly unbuttoning her blouse. She peeled away the fabric, revealing Jasmine's flushed skin beneath.

"Beautiful," Samantha whispered against Jasmine's collarbone, kissing a trail down to the valley of her breasts.

Jasmine's breath hitched, and she threaded her fingers through Samantha's hair, guiding her with silent pleas. The air grew thick with arousal as they continued to undress each other, each discarded garment a testament to their growing need. Jasmine's body was exquisite in the dim light, her skin glowing with a warmth that invited Samantha's touch, her exploration.

Her eyes flickered with lustful admiration, drinking in the sight of Jasmine in all her unadorned glory.

"Sam," Jasmine's voice broke through the heavy silence, laced with a desperate longing that mirrored Samantha's burning need. Their gazes locked, raw emotion churning within their eyes, an electric connection that sparked between them like a live wire.

"Yes?" Samantha responded, her voice nothing more than a low growl. Their bodies were inches apart, heat radiating off them in intoxicating waves. She watched as Jasmine's eyes darted down to her lips and back up again, a silent plea that she was only too happy to grant.

Tangling her fingers into Jasmine's hair, she pulled the other woman into a searing kiss. Their bodies moved together in a dance as old as time itself; a dance of desire and passion, surrender and claim. Their skin was warm where it touched, electrified by the chemistry that flowed between them.

Jasmine whimpered into the kiss, hands clawing at Samantha's back as she pressed herself closer. She could feel Samantha's pulse beneath her touch, rapid and wild just like her own.

"Are you sure?" Jasmine gasped as Samantha's fingertips grazed over the waistband of her skirt.

"More than ever," Samantha assured her, her eyes blazing with an intensity that left no room for doubt. With a swift movement, she removed the last barrier between them, and they stood there, bared to each other's hungry gaze.

"Touch me, Jasmine," Samantha commanded softly, offering her body as both a gift and a challenge.

And Jasmine did, her hands exploring Samantha's form with a reverence that soon turned to urgency. They tumbled onto the bed, limbs entwining, mouths seeking flesh. Their lovemaking was a dance of passion and discovery, each touch and moan a note in a symphony of pleasure. Samantha felt herself getting lost in the sensation, in the heat of Jasmine's skin against her own.

Samantha couldn't wait to see Jasmine's body transform, but she had to take her time. Her fingers found Jasmine's swollen clit and she began to apply gentle pressure, watching with rapt attention as Jasmine's breath hitched and her eyes fluttered shut in pleasure. "Sam," Jasmine gasped, her fingers digging into Samantha's arm. Samantha loved hearing her name on Jasmine's lips and longed to hear it again.

In response, she increased the tempo, feeling Jasmine's body tensing up beneath her touch. The air was filled with the sounds of their labored breathing and soft whimpers of pleasure. Every gasp and moan sent a jolt of arousal through Samantha, urging her on to bring Jasmine to the pinnacle of pleasure.

"There you go," Samantha murmured, her voice husky with desire as she felt Jasmine's body begin to tremble under her touch. She leaned down and captured Jasmine's lips in a passionate kiss.

She reveled in the taste of Jasmine's gasp, the way her body arched in ecstasy, the way she murmured Samantha's name over and over as waves of pleasure coursed through her. Samantha let her fingers move languidly, delighting in the shudders that swept through Jasmine's body.

The crescendo of their passion was building, a storm on the horizon that promised to sweep them both into its fervent embrace. As Jasmine's breaths came in shorter gasps, her body arching instinctively, Samantha could feel the precipice they were teetering upon.

"Sam... I can't—" Jasmine's words broke off in a whimper as she tried to pull away, the overwhelming sensations causing panic to flicker across her flushed features.

"No, stay with me," Samantha said firmly, pinning Jasmine gently but with undeniable strength beneath her. "I know what you're afraid of—the power inside you that's begging for release. I know you never had an orgasm, poor creature. Trust me, Jasmine. I will show you the way."

Jasmine's dark eyes met Samantha's blue ones, a silent conversation flowing between them. With a shaky exhale, Jasmine nodded, surrendering to the experience, to Samantha's guiding touch.

"Let it happen," Samantha whispered, her lips trailing kisses down Jasmine's neck, feeling the rapid pulse beneath her mouth.

With a final thrust of passion, Samantha encouraged Jasmine towards the edge, and with a strangled cry, Jasmine's body tensed, gripped by the throes of orgasm. But this was no ordinary climax; Samantha watched, fascinated, as Jasmine's body morphed before her eyes. From the apex of Jasmine's womanhood, an impressive cock unfurled, growing to its full, magnificent length.

"Fuck," Jasmine breathed out, her voice a mixture of awe and confusion as she looked down at herself, her hands instinctively reaching to touch the new part of her anatomy. The flesh was warm, pulsating with each beat of her heart—a physical manifestation of her futa nature now fully awakened.

"Beautiful," Samantha murmured, her own arousal spiking at the sight. She had witnessed this transformation many times before, yet it never ceased to amaze her—the raw power of the futa awakening.

"Is this... real?" Jasmine's question was laced with wonder, her fingers wrapping around her newfound girth, a moan slipping from her lips as she felt the sensitivity that rivaled any pleasure she had known before.

"Very real," Samantha confirmed, her gaze locked onto the magnificent erection before her. "And it's all yours, Jasmine. You've been chosen for this gift. And now, we're going to explore just how incredible it can be."

"Chosen?" Jasmine's voice wavered, her mind struggling to grasp the situation. "What do you mean? What am I?"

"Jasmine," Samantha started, "you're a futa—a woman graced with both femininity and masculinity. It's a rare and beautiful duality that few experience." She leaned closer, her blue eyes intense, locking onto Jasmine's bewildered brown gaze. "You have the power to give pleasure in ways most can only dream of."

Jasmine's breathing deepened as the truth settled within her, the weight of her cock a reminder of the change she had undergone. The fear that once gripped her was slowly being replaced by curiosity—and an undeniable excitement.

"But now," Samantha continued, her hand reaching out to gently stroke the length of Jasmine's cock, eliciting a sharp intake of breath from the newly awakened futa, "it's time for you to learn just how much pleasure you can provide." Samantha's touch was confident, assertive, her fingers tracing the veins that pulsed along Jasmine's shaft. "And I'll be your first. I want you to fuck me, Jasmine."

"Fuck you?" Jasmine echoed, the words foreign on her tongue, yet they ignited a fire deep within her core. Her body instinctively responded to Samantha's command, her cock twitching with anticipation.

"Yes," Samantha said, her lips curving into a seductive smile. "I demand it as a reward for guiding you through this awakening. You're going to fill me up with that gorgeous cock of yours. And I promise, it will be as good for you as it will be for me."

Jasmine froze up for a moment and Samantha realized that there was still some work left for her to do.

"Let me help you relax first," Samantha whispered as she knelt before Jasmine. She spread Jasmine's legs with her hands, appreciating the full view of her glistening folds. "You're so shy, my sweet futa. Let's get you warmed up."

"Samantha..." Jasmine's voice quivered, uncertainty laced with an edge of desire.

"Shh, just feel," Samantha cooed, leaning in to press her lips gently against Jasmine's pussy lips. Her tongue darted out, tasting the sweetness of Jasmine's arousal. As she licked and sucked at the tender flesh, her hand continued its dance along Jasmine's impressive length—the juxtaposition of soft and hard, gentle and firm, driving Jasmine towards the brink of madness.

"God, Sam... What is this feeling?" Jasmine gasped, her hips bucking into the dual sensation. Her hand found its way to Samantha's head, guiding her with a newfound boldness.

"Relax and enjoy it," Samantha said between laps, her own arousal growing. She savored the musky taste of Jasmine's cock as her mouth enveloped the head, her tongue swirling around it. With each stroke of her hand and flick of her tongue, Jasmine's moans grew louder, more fervent.

"Fuck, I'm... I can't believe how good this feels!" Jasmine cried out, her restraint crumbling under the onslaught of pleasure. "I've never felt anything like this!"

"Your body was made for this," Samantha murmured against Jasmine's throbbing cock, her words vibrating through the shaft. She increased the pace, sucking harder, her fingers deftly plunging inside Jasmine's dripping cunt. The room was filled with the wet sounds of Samantha's mouth working Jasmine's erection and Jasmine's pussy clenching around her probing fingers.

"Sam, I'm going to... I can't hold back!" Jasmine warned, her body tensing.

"Cum, Jasmine, fill me with sperm. Give it all to me," Samantha urged, her gaze locked on Jasmine's contorted face.

With a primal scream, Jasmine surrendered to the building pressure. Her cock exploded, hot streams of cum shooting into Samantha's eager mouth. It felt surreal and divine and utterly world-shattering all at once. Her body convulsed with the force of her climax, each throb of her cock drawing out her pleasure until she was drained but deliciously spent.

"Swallow it," Jasmine heard herself command, her voice thick with satisfaction. Samantha complied readily, swallowing down the copious load before pulling back to gaze up at Jasmine with a smug grin.

"I always knew you were a quick study," Samantha praised, standing up and wiping the corners of her mouth. Her gaze ran over Jasmine's exhausted form with patent desire. "But even I didn't expect that."

Jasmine's heart pounded in the aftermath of her orgasm, each beat echoing through her cock and sending aftershocks of pleasure through her. She looked down at Samantha, her breath hitching as she saw the lustful gleam in those blue eyes.

"I... I don't know what just happened," Jasmine confessed, her voice shaky.

Samantha chuckled warmly at the confession before climbing back onto the bed to sit beside Jasmine, their bodies warm against one another. "It's okay," she murmured soothingly, tracing idle patterns on Jasmine's thigh. "This is only the beginning," Samantha replied with a carnal smirk. "Now you know the power you wield. And you're going to use it to fuck me senseless."

Samantha's voice was a low purr as she turned her body around, positioning herself on all fours. Her back arched invitingly, presenting the round swell of her ass to Jasmine.

Jasmine's eyes were wide, pupils dilated with desire. "Yes... yes, I want more," she breathed, her voice trembling, her cum-smeared cock still hard.

"Good," Samantha replied, glancing over her shoulder with a sultry gaze.

Jasmine hesitated for only a moment before instinct took over. She approached Samantha, her hands reaching out to grip the seductive curves laid bare before her. As she positioned her newly grown cock at the entrance of Samantha's waiting pussy, a surge of primal energy coursed through her veins.

"Like this?" Jasmine asked, sliding into Samantha's warmth with one smooth thrust.

"Exactly like that," Samantha gasped, feeling the full length of Jasmine's cock filling her. The walls of her pussy clenched around Jasmine, pulling her deeper.

Jasmine found a rhythm, each thrust sending shockwaves of pleasure through both their bodies. Her hand landed on Samantha's ass, delivering a sharp slap that echoed in the room and left a red imprint on Samantha's skin.

"Fuck! Do that again," Samantha demanded, her voice laced with arousal.

Emboldened, Jasmine slapped her harder, grabbed a fistful of dark hair, and pulled, exposing the nape of Samantha's neck. Her hips moved with a fervor she'd never known she possessed, driving her cock into Samantha's cunt with relentless force.

"Is this how you like it?" Jasmine growled, surprised by the roughness in her own voice.

"Harder," Samantha instructed, pushing back against Jasmine's thrusts. "Make me feel it."

Jasmine began pounding Samantha brutally and it came so natural to her that she was taken aback by her own strength. She had always been the shy one, but now, she was the dominant. Samantha's moans of pleasure only spurred her on, infusing her with a primal need that left her breathless and wanting more.

Her strokes became wilder, faster. Each thrust was punctuated with a grunt of effort, a symphony of sounds that echoed through the room—skin against skin, labored breathing, Samantha's whimpers of pleasure.

"Fuck, Jasmine," Samantha gasped. "You're...you're..."

"Shhh," Jasmine hushed her, delivering another slap to Samantha's backside. "No words."

Samantha simply nodded, surrendering to Jasmine's powerful strokes. Her body shook under Jasmine's onslaught, her knees buckling until she was laying flat on the bed with Jasmine over her. But that didn't stop Jasmine; if anything, it lent her an advantage. She gripped Samantha's hips and pounded into her relentlessly from behind.

The sight of Samantha's ass jiggling with each thrust sent more blood rushing to Jasmine's eager cock.

But she wanted more.

Flipping Samantha onto her back without breaking contact, Jasmine now hovered above her, looking down into those piercing blue eyes that sparkled with lustful challenge. She admired the way Samantha's breasts bounced with each powerful thrust, the way her nipples stiffened, begging for attention.

"God, you're fucking gorgeous," Jasmine praised, her words dripping with carnal appreciation. She leaned down to capture a nipple between her fingers, pinching firmly, eliciting a sharp intake of breath from Samantha.

"More," Samantha moaned, her hands reaching up to tangle in Jasmine's curls. "I need more."

Jasmine's hand wrapped around Samantha's throat, applying gentle pressure. Samantha's eyes rolled back in ecstasy, her body responding to every assertion of Jasmine's dominance.

"Tell me how much you love it," Jasmine commanded, her thrusts becoming more erratic as her own pleasure mounted.

"More than anything," Samantha managed to gasp out, the edges of her vision blurring with the intensity of the sensations coursing through her. "You're incredible, Jasmine. Fuck me. Own me."

"Jump for me, Samantha. Show me how bad you want it," Jasmine growled, her hands roaming over Samantha's sweat-slicked skin, each touch igniting a new fire within.

Samantha obliged, lifting herself up only to impale herself back down onto Jasmine's pulsating cock. The room echoed with the wet sounds of their union and Samantha's moans. "Your cock... it fills me up so perfectly," she panted, the raw hunger in her voice matching the wildness in Jasmine's eyes.

"Fuck, yes," Jasmine hissed, her grip on Samantha's hips tightening. "You're such a hot little slut for this futa dick."

"Fuck," Samantha shot back, her movements growing more frantic as she sought that peak that loomed just out of reach. Each word they exchanged was a stroke against the tinder of their arousal, sparking flames that threatened to devour their flesh.

"Still not fast enough?" Samantha challenged, her breathing heavy with exertion and excitement.

With a primal grunt, Jasmine stood, lifting Samantha effortlessly. She pinned her against the wall, her powerful thrusts now unrelenting. The force of her body drove Samantha upward, only to be caught again by Jasmine's relentless desire.

"Jasmine!" Samantha cried out, her nails digging into the other woman's shoulders as she felt the crescendo of pleasure building within her. "I'm close..."

"Fuck, I'm going to fill you so good," Jasmine rasped, her voice thick with lust. Her cock swelled further inside Samantha, signaling the imminent explosion.

As if on cue, they both tumbled over the edge. Samantha's whole body tensed, her pussy clenching around Jasmine's cock like a vice as waves of orgasmic bliss crashed over her. Her vision whited out, and for a moment, there was nothing but pure ecstasy.

Jasmine's release followed immediately after, her cock throbbing as it released its load deep within Samantha, marking her cunt. A guttural moan escaped her lips as her knees nearly buckled under the intensity of the orgasm, the world narrowing down to the incredible sensation of emptying herself into Samantha again and again.

They clung to each other, Jasmine's cock softening inside Samantha but still nestled within her warmth. In the aftermath of their cataclysmic orgasms, their rapid heartbeats slowly returned to normal, their sweat-mingled bodies sliding gently against one another in tender caresses.

"Samantha, thank you... I feel complete, whole, finally..."

Samantha smirked. "This is what I do."

"Can I fuck you tomorrow?"

"Sorry Jasmine, but tomorrow I am going to the gym."

The End.

Futa Hunter: Yoga Teacher

Samantha took of her shoes and stepped on the bamboo floor of the Asana Ascendancy Yoga Studio, a prestigious haven for those seeking inner peace within the city's hustle. The receptionist's smile was as serene as the Buddha statue gracing the lobby. Samantha signed up for a private session, her gaze catching the glint of sunlight that danced through the fluttering white curtains framing the studio's floor-to-ceiling windows.

"Your instructor will be Zoe Mitchell," the receptionist informed her, handing over a form.

"Perfect."

Zoe entered, her platinum hair a stark contrast against the earthy tones of the room. "Welcome to Asana Ascendancy. I'm Zoe," she said, extending a lithe hand.

"Delighted," Samantha purred, the thrill of the hunt igniting in her veins as she recognized an uninitiated futa. She usually had to put effort in order to find one, yet here she was, walking right into her web. Samantha smiled, grasping Zoe's hand and holding it a breath longer than necessary.

"Let's begin with some deep breathing," Zoe suggested, her voice maintaining professional warmth.

"Breathing... I can think of a few activities that would have me panting," Samantha said, eyeing Zoe's petite frame with undisguised desire.

Zoe chuckled nervously, adjusting the strap of her tank top. "Right. Well, focus on channeling your energy through your body." She demonstrated a slow inhale, chest rising, then exhaling deeply.

"Channel my energy? I prefer to channel my energy into more... stimulating pursuits," Samantha replied, leaning closer to catch Zoe's scent—a mix of lavender and something wilder, an untapped sensuality waiting beneath the surface.

"Uh, sure," Zoe muttered, cheeks coloring slightly as she guided Samantha into a standing mountain pose. "From here, let's transition into a forward fold. Let gravity pull you down."

"Gravity's not the only thing pulling me right now," Samantha murmured, bending forward and casting a glance back at Zoe, her eyes smoldering like blue flames.

"Try to keep your mind on the practice," Zoe advised, hands gently pressing on Samantha's lower back to deepen the stretch, unaware of the fire she was stoking within her student.

"Your touch is quite... skilled. Do you use it often?" Samantha teased, allowing a soft moan to slip from her lips as Zoe's fingers traced the curve of her spine.

"Only professionally," Zoe replied, though her voice wavered, betraying a growing awareness of the charged atmosphere.

"Such a shame," Samantha sighed, straightening up and stepping closer to Zoe, so close she could feel the heat radiating from her body. "I can imagine your hands working wonders on me," she breathed out.

Zoe swallowed hard, her blue eyes flashing a momentary wildness before she regained her composure. "Well, yoga does wonders for the body... Let's continue."

"Lead the way," Samantha said, her heart pounding with anticipation. She knew the dance well—the slow seduction, the inevitable surrender. And as Zoe moved to demonstrate the next position, Samantha followed, poised to ensnare her unsuspecting prey.

"Next, we'll move into Anjaneyasana, the low lunge," Zoe instructed, demonstrating with grace. Her movements were fluid, a dance of strength and flexibility that Samantha admired with an appreciative gaze.

"Like this?" Samantha asked, positioning her leg forward, knee bent, and stretching her other leg back, sinking her hips down towards the mat. She felt Zoe's hands on her hips, gently correcting her alignment.

"Exactly, just make sure to engage your core," Zoe said, her voice soft but professional. However, Samantha caught the slight hitch in her breath as her hands lingered a little longer than necessary.

"Engage my core, got it," Samantha echoed. She tilted her head back slightly, offering Zoe a view of her neck, exposed and vulnerable. "What's next?"

"From here, we transition into Ardha Chandrasana, the half moon pose." Zoe's demonstration was seamless, her petite frame balancing effortlessly as she lifted one leg parallel to the floor and reached skyward with the opposite arm.

"Balance and openness," Samantha mused aloud, mimicking the position with a deliberate sensuality. She faltered intentionally, reaching out to grasp Zoe's shoulder for support.

"Steady now," Zoe cautioned, her hand wrapping around Samantha's waist to stabilize her. The contact sent a jolt of electricity through them both, lingering like a promise of more to come.

"Thank you," Samantha breathed, her eyes locking with Zoe's, "for being so supportive."

"It's what I'm here for," Zoe replied, with a quiver in her voice. Their gazes held, charged with unspoken desire, and for a moment, there was nothing else in the world but the two of them—teacher and student, hunter and prey, drawn together by an irresistible force.

"Shall we... move on?" Zoe asked, her cheeks flushed with a rosy hue that Samantha found utterly captivating.

"Let's," Samantha responded, her own voice husky with anticipation. Zoe gracefully demonstrated the next sequence, her body contorted into a challenging Eagle pose. The two women were in such close proximity that their breaths became intertwined, creating a powerful energy between them.

The floorboards creaked softly beneath them as they shifted from one pose to another. The room was warm, the air thick with the musk of exertion and something far more primal. Samantha could see the flush in Zoe's cheeks deepening, a rosy hue that she found utterly captivating.

"Your body is so responsive," Samantha complimented, her hands boldly tracing the lines of Zoe's form as she aided in the transitions. "It's like you were made for this."

Zoe's reply was cut short by a sharp intake of breath as Samantha's touch ventured dangerously close to the heat between her thighs. "Samantha..." she warned, but there was no conviction behind the word.

"Call me Sam," Samantha urged, her lips ghosting over Zoe's ear. "Everyone does once they get to know me better."

"Sam," Zoe repeated, her voice barely above a whisper. The intimacy of using her name seemed to break down another barrier, and Samantha knew she had her right where she wanted.

The yoga studio, with its serene atmosphere and muted sounds, became their sanctuary—a place where the awakening was about to unfold. Samantha could feel the hunger building within Zoe, a mirror to her own predatory need. The thrill of the hunt was reaching its crescendo, and she relished every moment, ready to claim her reward.

"Can't focus on the poses anymore?" Samantha teased, brushing her fingertips along Zoe's collarbone and down to the scoop of her sports bra.

"Yoga is about connection... with oneself," Zoe managed to say, though her breath hitched as Samantha's hands cupped her breasts through the fabric.

"Then let's connect," Samantha whispered, leaning in to press a soft kiss to Zoe's lips.

The kiss was gentle at first, lips barely touching, but it soon deepened with an intensity that left them both breathless. As they pulled away, their eyes locked, and without a word, they began to undress each other.

Samantha's fingers deftly worked the knot of Zoe's top, peeling the damp fabric away to reveal pale, smooth skin that begged to be touched. She kissed her way down Zoe's neck, savoring the salty taste of sweat that clung to her.

"Beautiful," Samantha murmured against the hollow of Zoe's throat, her hands exploring the newly bared flesh.

Zoe's small, yet firm breasts stood proudly, her nipples hardening under Samantha's gaze. "You're stunning, Sam," Zoe said, her hands mimicking the movements on Samantha's body, pulling her tank top over her head and tossing it aside.

Samantha's own ample curves were released, her dark hair cascading over her shoulders as Zoe's gaze devoured her. Zoe leaned forward, taking one of Samantha's nipples into her mouth, eliciting a soft moan from her lips.

"God, your mouth feels incredible," Samantha gasped, threading her fingers through Zoe's platinum blonde hair.

As the last of their clothing fell to the mat, their bodies came together in a rush of skin on skin. Samantha's curvaceous form pressed against Zoe's leaner one, each curve molding into the other's dips and valleys.

"Your skin is like silk," Zoe breathed out, her hands sliding over Samantha's ass, squeezing the firm flesh appreciatively.

"More," Samantha demanded, her hips arching into Zoe's touch. "I want to feel all of you."

They kissed again, deeper, hungrier, their hands roaming each other's bodies with abandon. Samantha lavished Zoe's neck with kisses, trailing down to capture a nipple between her teeth gently, drawing a sharp intake of breath and a whimper from Zoe.

"Fuck, Sam, don't stop," Zoe pleaded, her back arching off the mat, pushing her breast further into Samantha's mouth.

With each caress the air around them crackled with electricity.

"Zoe," Samantha whispered against the flushed skin of her instructor's stomach, "I want to taste you."

Zoe's breath hitched. "Yes, please," she managed, her body tensing with need as Samantha slid down her lithe form.

Settling between Zoe's spread thighs, Samantha admired the sight before her. She licked her lips, savoring the moment, knowing that Zoe was on the brink of an earth-shattering transformation. Soon, so very soon she will be the first one to taste Zoe's new cock.

With one long, languorous lick, she savored the sweetness of Zoe's arousal, eliciting a soft moan from above.

"Sam..." Zoe's voice trembled, and Samantha could feel the tension coiling within her, the energy of an unawakened futa ready to surge forth.

"Relax, let go," Samantha murmured, sliding two fingers inside Zoe's slick pussy, setting a rhythm that had Zoe writhing beneath her.

"Something... something's happening," Zoe gasped, her body beginning to tense unnaturally.

Samantha felt it too, a pulsing energy emanating from Zoe's core. "It's okay, beautiful. Let it happen," she reassured, even as she pinned Zoe's hands beside her head, asserting control.

Zoe's eyes widened in a mix of fear and exhilaration. "I can't—"

"Trust me," Samantha cut her off, her mouth returning to Zoe's clit, her tongue working in tandem with her fingers. She could sense the hesitation in Zoe's quivering muscles, but she wouldn't allow Zoe to retreat from her destiny.

"Sam!" Zoe cried out, her back arching off the mat, as the sensation within her reached a crescendo.

Samantha doubled her efforts, her tongue and fingers moving with purpose, coaxing Zoe toward the point of no return.

Zoe's breaths came in ragged gasps, her body trembling on the edge of release. "I'm—" The words broke off into a strangled cry as the transformation began, a powerful orgasm ripping through her.

"Let it happen," Samantha breathed against Zoe's throbbing clit, not relenting for a second.

"Fuck—Sam!" Zoe's orgasm crashed over her like a tidal wave, her entire being consumed by pleasure so intense it bordered on pain.

As Zoe's climax continued to shudder through her, Samantha finally released her grip, watching with satisfaction as Zoe rode out the waves of her first awakened release, a pivotal moment in the life of every futa. Her dark hair fanned out around her as she watched the spectacle unfold before her with a mixture of awe and desire. Zoe's eyes were wide with shock, her lips parted in a silent scream as the impossible happened. From between her legs, where Samantha's fingers had been relentlessly stirring her depths, something new and magnificent emerged.

"Sam..." Zoe's voice was a breathless whisper, tinged with disbelief. Her hands moved instinctively towards the burgeoning length, her touch tentative at first, then surging with wonder as her fingers wrapped around the throbbing girth of her newly formed cock. "What's happening to me?"

"Welcome to your true self, Zoe," Samantha said. She rose to her knees, her piercing blue eyes locked onto Zoe's massive dick, her own pussy clenching in anticipation. "You're a futa now."

"A futa?" Zoe echoed, her gaze still fixated on the impressive organ that seemed to pulse with its own heartbeat, growing ever more solid in her grasp.

"Exactly." Samantha's lips curled into a predatory smile. "A woman blessed with both sets of pleasure-giving tools." She crawled closer, her movements deliberate, exuding confidence. "And now, you're going to fuck me as a reward for awakening you to this ecstasy."

Zoe's breathing hitched, her mind reeling from the rush of sensations that accompanied her new appendage. She felt powerful, emboldened by the weight and heat of it against her palm. "I—I don't know how..." Uncertainty flickered across her face, but Samantha was quick to dispel it.

"Trust me, your body knows exactly what to do," Samantha said, her hand reaching out to stroke Zoe's cheek, guiding her to look up from her lap and into Samantha's hungry eyes. "Just let your instincts take over."

The air was thick with the scent of arousal as Samantha guided Zoe's hand, showing her how to stroke herself, building the tension, the desire. Zoe's hips bucked involuntarily, a moan escaping her lips as she realized just how sensitive she was, every touch amplified to an exquisite degree.

"Wow," Zoe uttered, a sense of wonder lacing her panting breaths as she adjusted to the weighty presence pulsating between her thighs. "It feels... so natural." She marveled, her eyes wide with both shock and excitement. Her entire body seemed to resonate with an unfamiliar yet astounding energy.

"Natural, huh?" Samantha's voice was a velvet purr, her gaze locked onto Zoe's newly adorned anatomy with unabashed fascination. "I told you, you were born for this."

Zoe nodded slowly, absorbing the truth of Samantha's words. For years, she'd sought the kind of spiritual equilibrium that yoga promised, the balance that had always eluded her. But now, as her chi coursed through her in powerful, unimpeded waves, she understood what true harmony felt like. It resonated from her core, vibrating through her cock with each throb of awakened flesh.

"Sam," Zoe began, her voice a mix of awe and caution, "this is incredible, but we can't rush this. I need to explore... to understand."

Samantha chuckled softly, rolling onto her back, exposing the glistening invitation of her pussy. "Then explore me," she invited huskily, spreading her legs in blatant offer.

Without hesitation, Zoe lowered herself, her tongue tentatively reaching out to taste Samantha's cunt. The salty-sweetness of arousal on her palate spurred her on, and she began to lap eagerly at Samantha's clit, savoring the sultry moan that spilled from above.

"Mmm, yes, just like that," Samantha breathed, her fingers tangling into Zoe's short platinum locks, guiding her rhythmically. Desire sparked within, fanning the flames that Zoe's tongue had kindled.

As Zoe's confidence grew, she introduced her fingers, sliding them into Samantha's velvety warmth. She felt Samantha clench around her digits, her own cock twitching in response to the perfect connection.

"Fuck, Zoe..." Samantha's voice broke on a high note as her hips lifted off the mat to meet Zoe's thrusts. A symphony of pleasure cascaded through her, her blue eyes darkening like the depths of a stormy sea.

"Tell me what you need," Zoe whispered against the slick folds she was so attentively worshiping, her breath hot against Samantha's engorged clit.

"More," came the desperate reply, tinged with an edge of command. Samantha's world narrowed to the exquisite pressure building inside her, the heat of Zoe's mouth on her sensitive flesh.

Zoe obliged, curling her fingers in that special way, hitting the spot that made Samantha arch her back and cry out. The sound of it vibrated straight to Zoe's core, her own arousal mirroring Samantha's crescendo.

"Zoe!" Samantha gasped, the dam breaking as waves of orgasm crashed over her. Her body shuddered with release, her inner muscles fluttering around Zoe's fingers in sweet spasms. It was divine, transcendent, and yet, it wasn't enough.

"Again," Samantha demanded, her breathing ragged, her lust far from satiated. "More!"

"Can you handle more, Samantha?" Zoe's voice was thick with arousal, her blue eyes locking onto Samantha's.

"Fuck, yes," Samantha breathed out, a lustful smirk playing on her lips. She eyed Zoe's newly manifested cock, its impressive girth calling to her like a siren's song. "I want to taste you."

"Fuck, yes," Zoe murmured, the anticipation making her flesh tremble. She watched as Samantha shifted her position, her long, dark hair cascading over her shoulders as she descended.

Samantha wrapped her lips around Zoe's cock, and an involuntary moan escaped Zoe's throat. The warmth, the wetness—it was divine. Her hips bucked instinctively, seeking more of that perfect sensation. She concentrated on her breathing, deep and controlled, a technique she'd often used in yoga to enhance her spiritual experiences. Now it served to heighten her sexual ecstasy, turning every lick, every suck into waves of pleasure that threatened to wash her away.

"Your mouth... it's incredible," Zoe gasped, fingers threading through Samantha's hair, guiding her rhythmically. She felt the peak approaching fast, a tidal wave of ecstasy building at the base of her spine.

Samantha worked fervently, her tongue swirling around the head of Zoe's cock, drawing out each thread of pleasure.

Samantha felt a surge of power. This was her domain, where she was most alive—the hunt, the seduction, the victory. She rose above Zoe, straddling her, the heat of their bodies mingling. She positioned herself over Zoe's still-throbbing cock, her pussy slick with anticipation. Lowering herself onto her, both women groaned at the exquisite fullness.

"Ride me, Samantha. Show me how much you want it," Zoe pleaded, her hands reaching up to grasp Samantha's swaying breasts.

With a fierce determination, Samantha began to move, her hips grinding down onto Zoe in a relentless rhythm. Each slap against Zoe's flesh, each pinch and twist of her nipples, each gentle choke only fueled the fire within them.

"Like this?" Samantha taunted between gasps, her control absolute even as she lost herself in the sensation. "Is this what your chi wanted?"

"Fuck, yes," Zoe managed to say, her voice strained with pleasure. "This is energy... this is balance."

Zoe's futa cock stretched Samantha impossibly, every thrust meeting her deepest spots. Their breaths grew ragged, their bodies slick with sweat as they raced towards climax.

"Harder, Zoe," Samantha hissed through gritted teeth. She could feel the pressure building inside her, that sweet knot of ecstasy that promised to unravel her entirely. The tip of Zoe's cock brushed against her sweet spot with each thrust, sending sparks of pleasure coursing through her.

Zoe complied, gripping Samantha's waist tightly as she drove into her over and over again.

They fell into sync, moving together in a rhythm that seemed as natural as breathing, each thrust meeting the other's body with sublime precision.

Samantha leaned forward, capturing Zoe's lips in a passionate kiss that matched the fervor of their bodies. Zoe tasted herself on Samantha's mouth: a heady cocktail of lust and possession that made her moan.

The friction between their bodies built up to a crescendo, their sweaty bodies slipping and sliding against each other. Their moans filled the room as they chased after their climax, lost in each other.

Samantha could feel her own pleasure mounting again, spurred on by Zoe's responses. Her movements grew more desperate, more insistent, as she sought her own release atop Zoe's powerful form.

But then, with a sudden surge of energy that seemed to emanate from her very core, Zoe's expression morphed into one of feral intensity. "My chi... it's too much," she gasped, her breaths coming in short, sharp pants as the mystical life force within her threatened to overwhelm.

"Let it go," Samantha whispered, her voice almost drowned by the thundering of her own heartbeat. She could feel Zoe's body tensing beneath her, the muscles coiling like springs.

"Fuck chi!" Zoe exclaimed, and with a strength that took Samantha by surprise, she was flipped onto her back. Her head hit the soft yoga mat with a gentle thud, and before she could catch her breath, Zoe was upon her, entering her with a fierce thrust that robbed Samantha of words.

"Zoe—" she tried to speak, but all that came out was a moan, high and keening, as Zoe began to move with a brutal rhythm that tapped into something wild and unfettered.

"Feel me, Samantha," Zoe growled, her hips snapping forward again and again, each movement a testament to the power coursing through her newly awakened cock. "This is what it means to be alive!"

As Zoe fucked her, Samantha's world narrowed to the point of pleasure that spiraled deep within her. Every thrust sent shockwaves through her body, building up an orgasm that promised to eclipse all others. Her fingers clawed at the mat, seeking purchase, as her legs wrapped around Zoe's waist, urging her on.

"Harder, Zoe! Don't you dare stop!" Samantha cried out, lost in the tempest of sensation.

She leaned down, her breasts brushing against Samantha's with every movement, her lips trailing kisses along Samantha's jawline, marking her skin with the heat of her breath.

The room seemed to vibrate with the force of their coupling, the air heavy with the scent of sex and sweat. Samantha's thoughts fragmented, unable to form anything coherent beyond the need, the desire, the sheer ecstasy that Zoe was driving her towards.

"Come for me, Samantha. Now!" Zoe commanded, picking up the pace even more, relentless and unyielding.

And Samantha did come, her orgasm ripping through her like a hurricane, leaving her gasping and trembling beneath Zoe. But even as the waves of pleasure receded, she could see in Zoe's eyes that she was far from satisfied.

"More," Zoe panted, her voice hoarse with desire. "I need more."

Without a moment's respite, Zoe's hands gripped Samantha's hips, flipping her onto her stomach effortlessly. The cool air of the studio contrasted sharply with the heat radiating from their entwined bodies as Zoe positioned herself behind Samantha, her fingers tracing the curve of her ass before aligning her throbbing cock with Samantha's waiting entrance.

Zoe entered her slowly at first, allowing Samantha to adjust to the new angle, the stretch almost unbearable. Then, with a steadiness that belied the frenzy of their previous coupling, she began to move, each thrust deeper, harder, more insistent than the last. The pounding was relentless, each stroke of Zoe's cock inside Samantha sending waves of pleasure coursing through her body. Her desire was a living thing, a tangible entity that enveloped them both.

Samantha felt Zoe's hand creep under her, finding her clit and rubbing circles around it. Samantha let out a loud moan as the pleasure doubled, radiating from both her front and back. Each thrust slammed into her, resonating in places she had never known existed. Her hands clutched at the mat beneath her desperately as Zoe continued to pound her so very hard.

"God, yes... Zoe, you're incredible," Samantha managed between gasps, feeling Zoe's hands tighten around her hips, anchoring her against the powerful thrusts.

"Fuck, Samantha... You feel so good," Zoe panted, her thrusts growing erratic as she neared her own edge. "I'm close."

"Me too," Samantha confessed, her body tensing in delicious anticipation of release.

Their movements became frenzied, desperate, racing toward that climactic precipice together. And then it hit—a cosmic orgasm that seemed to stretch time and space, a supernova of sensation that erupted from within them both. Samantha cried out, her voice a raw testament to the intensity of her climax, feeling Zoe's cock pulsing inside her as she reached her own shattering release. Zoe's very first ejaculation felt like liquid fire, its hot warmth filling Samantha to the brim. The rhythmic spasms of Zoe's cock caused a pleasurable aftershock that sent Samantha into another round of climax, her cries mixing with Zoe's in a chorus of ecstasy.

Zoe's body shook with the force of it, a primal part of her reveling in the act of filling Samantha. Overwhelmed by it all, she collapsed on top of Samantha, their bodies damp with sweat and the evidence of their shared ecstasy.

"God, Zoe," Samantha gasped out, as she felt Zoe's weight atop her; a comforting presence despite the way her body still quaked from the aftershocks.

Zoe didn't reply verbally. Exhausted but content, she simply nuzzled into Samantha's neck, pressing soft kisses against the slick skin there. Her hand lazily trailed up and down Samantha's sides in a soothing gesture.

They lay there for what felt like hours — wrapped up in each other, their bodies sated from their dirty fucking.

Samantha turned her head to meet Zoe's eyes, seeing a mix of wonder and concern flicker across her features.

"Damn, how am I ever going to wear yoga pants with this huge dick now?" Zoe marveled, half-joking, half-serious as she glanced down at her still impressive erection.

Samantha laughed, a light, joyous sound that filled the room. "We'll figure it out. Maybe start a new trend?"

"Perhaps," Zoe said. "So, what are you doing tomorrow?"

"Resting, after today? Definitely resting," Samantha replied, her tone playful yet earnest, her body already anticipating the sweet ache that would come with morning.

The End.

Futa Hunter: Awakened

The twilight draped its serene shroud over the city as Samantha Carter strolled through the abandoned streets, her heels clicking in rhythmic solitude against the pavement. Exhaustion clung to her limbs with the tenacity of a second skin, born from the relentless hunt that had consumed her nights – a hunt that saw the awakening of futa after futa under her experienced guidance. With each step, the cool evening air brushed against her flushed cheeks, whispering promises of respite.

"Melissa," she murmured to herself, recalling the shy Spanish teacher's transformation, how her soft moans blossomed into cries of ecstasy. Samantha's lips curled into a sly smile as she imagined Chloe's lithe body writhing in pleasure, the way her green eyes had shimmered with newfound hunger. And Victoria, the supermodel whose haughty facade crumbled under Samantha's touch, revealing a fervor she never knew she possessed. And the others, so many others...

"Enough," Samantha chided herself, quelling the mounting heat within her. "Tonight is for me, no hunting, no awakening... just peace and quiet."

Her determined strides led her to the quaint glow of a small store at the corner, its neon sign a beacon for her planned sanctuary. The bell above the door jangled as she entered, the scent of buttery popcorn immediately enveloping her senses.

"Good evening," she greeted nonchalantly while scanning the aisles for the trifecta of her solo movie night: a chick flick, popcorn, and cola. Selecting a tear-jerker guaranteed to require a box of tissues, she scooped up a bag of kernels and reached for a chilled bottle.

"Will that be all for tonight?" The cashier, a woman with an unassuming air, smiled as she rang up the items.

"Unless you've got a magic potion to relieve sore muscles hidden behind that counter," Samantha flirted back, her tone light, playful.

"Sorry, fresh out of magic potions today," the cashier replied with a chuckle. "But if I come across one, you'll be the first to know."

"Make sure you do," Samantha winked, relieved that there was nothing otherworldly about this woman – no telltale aura of a futa waiting to be awakened. She wouldn't have to engage in another sensual chase tonight.

"Enjoy your movie night," the cashier called out as Samantha turned to leave, her arms cradling the paper bag with her chosen comforts.

"Thanks," she said, stepping back into the solitude of the street, the anticipation of a quiet evening soothing her like a balm. Tonight, the hunter would rest, surrounded by nothing more than the fiction of on-screen romance and the simple pleasure of being alone.

Samantha's steps echoed along the empty corridor leading to her apartment, her mind still wrapped in the cocoon of impending relaxation. But as she reached for her keys, a subtle dissonance struck her—the door was ajar, just barely, but enough to send a ripple of alarm through her.

She exhaled slowly, pushing down the unease that crept up her spine. She hadn't left in a rush; she wouldn't have forgotten to lock her door. Samantha slipped her hand into her purse, fingers wrapping around the familiar shape of her pepper spray, a silent sentinel in situations just like this.

Taking another breath, she nudged the door open with the tip of her boot, the faint creaking sound magnifying in the silence. Her heart thrummed against her ribs, a staccato beat that matched her cautious steps. The dimness of the living room swallowed her figure, shadows clinging to the walls like specters.

"Hello?" Her voice was a soft challenge to the quiet, a test to see if it would be answered by anything other than her own pulse.

A shuffling noise from deeper within the darkness drew her attention. It was soft, almost hesitant, but undeniably there. Samantha's grip on the pepper spray tightened.

"Who's there?" she demanded as she stepped further into her domain. Her free hand found the wall, fingers trailing along its surface until they brushed the light switch.

The click seemed to echo, a prelude to revelation, and then the room burst into light. Samantha blinked against the sudden brightness, spots dancing before her eyes. When her vision cleared, the sight that greeted her was beyond any scenario she had concocted.

There they were—eight figures standing in her living room, illuminated like deities of some hedonistic pantheon. Melissa, Ava, Chloe, Victoria, Emily, Sophia, Jasmine, and Zoe—all naked, all gloriously erect. Each body was a testament to the diversity of desire, from Melissa's gentle curves to Ava's fiery presence, Chloe's athletic grace to Victoria's towering elegance. Emily stood with a doctor's poise, her red curls a fiery halo, while Sophia's commanding figure exuded power. Jasmine's hidden sensuality was now on full display, and Zoe's playful energy vibrated through the air.

Eight beautiful futas and eight glorious, magnificent cocks.

"Surprise," they said in unison, their voices a sultry chorus that sent a thrill through Samantha. The reality of her former prey turned predators caused a delicious chill to run through her, even as her initial fear melted away under their hungry gazes.

"Did you miss me that much?" Samantha teased, her lips curving into a knowing smile. Her fingers relaxed around the canister of pepper spray, no longer needed among the futas she had helped blossom into their true selves.

"More than you know," Ava purred, her green eyes locked onto Samantha with an intensity that promised untold pleasures.

"Looks like my movie night just got a lot more interesting," Samantha quipped, her eyes roaming over the array of flesh before her—the jutting cocks, the firm breasts, the round asses. A different kind of hunger began to gnaw at her insides, one that no popcorn or soda could satisfy.

"Indeed," Victoria added, her voice dripping with anticipation. "We've got quite the feature presentation planned for you."

"Allow us to explain," Ava began, a coy grin playing on her lips as she leaned against the doorframe, her posture relaxed yet commanding. "We've found each other on the internet. I mean, the first thing each of us did was to try and find other futas in the city, so that is how we discovered each other and you as the woman linking all of us."

"An online forum for the newly initiated," Emily chimed in, her eyes sparkling with mischief. "A place where we could share our experiences, our transformations." She paused, looked directly at Samantha, and added, "And our insatiable hunger for the huntress who made us."

"Wait, you set up a futa forum?" Samantha asked. "Who would have thought? My little fledglings, all grown up and plotting together."

"Indeed," Jasmine confirmed, her soft smile a stark contrast to the lust in her eyes. "And then Ava, your generous landlord, decided it was time for a reunion, so she let us all in. So that all of us would have a chance for us to thank you properly."

"Thank me?" Samantha echoed, her voice thick with the anticipation that tightened her chest.

"By giving you exactly what you need," Zoe said, her playful tone belied by the earnestness in her gaze. "To be taken care of, for once. To be the center of our world, as you've made us the center of yours."

"Tonight is about you, Samantha," Sophia declared. "Your pleasure. Your release. Your reward."

"Reward?" Samantha tilted her head, feigning confusion even as the heat between her thighs betrayed her true feelings. "And how do you intend to give me this 'reward'?"

"By fucking you senseless," Chloe stated bluntly, the raw desire in her eyes echoing the sentiments of her sisters in cocks.

"Each of us owes you a debt of pleasure," Ava said, stepping closer, her hips swaying hypnotically. "And we intend to pay it back with interest."

Samantha's breathing quickened, her body responding instinctively to their words and the promise they held. She glanced at the bag in her hand, the contents now seeming trivial in comparison to the feast of flesh awaiting her.

"Bring it on," Samantha said, her voice thick with desire as she tossed the bag aside, the sound of scattering popcorn a mere footnote to the symphony of arousal that filled the room.

Samantha's heartbeat thrummed in her ears as the futas descended on her like a storm of sensuality. Eight pairs of hands reached for her with an eagerness that matched the hunger in their eyes. Fabric tore, buttons flew, and within moments, Samantha stood amidst the ruins of her clothing, her skin bared to the admiring gazes and eager touches of her worshippers.

"God, you're beautiful," Emily murmured, her lips tracing the curve of Samantha's shoulder, leaving a line of wet fire in their wake.

"Look at this ass," Ava praised, squeezing the firm flesh with a possessive grip that made Samantha shiver with delight. "Made for spanking."

Samantha couldn't help but arch into their caresses, the union of eight mouths and tongues exploring her ignited every nerve ending. Victoria's tongue painted delicate swirls around her navel, sending shudders through Samantha's core, while Jasmine's fingers danced over the sensitive skin along her inner thigh, teasingly close to where Samantha ached to be touched.

"Such perfect tits," Zoe sighed, circling Samantha's areolas with a thumb before leaning in to capture a nipple between her teeth, tugging just enough to elicit a gasp from Samantha's lips.

"Does our hunter like being hunted?" Melissa's voice was husky, her breath hot against Samantha's earlobe before she took it between her lips, laving it with her tongue.

Samantha's only response was to thread her fingers through Melissa's hair and pull her closer, her body language speaking volumes more than words could. Her mind was a haze of arousal, each touch stoking the fires that burned within her.

The room was a tableau of lust, a chaos of eight hard cocks standing at attention, eight pairs of breasts begging to be fondled, and eight juicy asses primed for slapping. Samantha's hands roamed freely, grabbing hold of whatever flesh she could reach, each stroke and slap punctuated by her breathy moans and the dirty encouragement she spat out.

"Fuck, your cocks are so hard for me...I want to feel every inch," Samantha growled, her hand wrapping around Sophia's shaft with a firmness that drew a groan from the futa's lips.

"Enjoying yourself?" Chloe asked, a smirk playing on her lips as Samantha's hand trailed down to cup her juicy ass.

"Immensely," Samantha panted, her eyes half-lidded with desire. "Don't think you'll get off easy. I want to see you all squirm for me too."

Their responses were a symphony of affirmative grunts and moans, their bodies a writhing mass of pleasure and need, all centered around the fulcrum that was Samantha. She reveled in the power she held, even as they worshiped her with their mouths and hands. It was a dynamic of give and take, a dance of dominance and submission where everyone led and followed in turn.

"Let us show you what true pleasure feels like," Sophia whispered.

And as the futas converged on her, hungry to fulfill their pledge of ecstasy, Samantha knew one thing for certain: tonight, she would be devoured completely—and she would savor every moment.

Melissa positioned herself between Samantha's spread legs, her hips grinding against the entrance to Samantha's wet pussy. With one swift motion, she thrust inside her, eliciting a gasp from Samantha as she felt every inch of Melissa's hard cock filling her up. The demure Spanish teacher pounded into Samantha with unexpected force, her brown eyes filled with lust and determination.

"God, you're so tight," Melissa moaned, her hands gripping Samantha's hips tightly. Samantha could only manage a breathless whimper in response, her mind reeling from the brutal pleasure.

Eager to join in, Ava stepped forward, her green eyes locked onto Samantha's lips. "Open wide," she commanded, stroking her thick shaft suggestively. Samantha complied without hesitation, opening her mouth to receive Ava's cock. The landlord shoved it in roughly, filling Samantha's throat with her pulsating member. Gagging slightly, Samantha focused on taking Ava's full length.

Samantha moaned around Ava's swollen cock, her eyes rolling into the back of her head as she tasted the salty tang mixed with arousal. She felt Melissa's dick pumping into her pussy, filling her up while Chloe's fingers teased her clit. Zoe sank to her knees, pressing her lips against Samantha's stomach, kissing the sensitive flesh. Jasmine teased Samantha's nipples, flicking them with her tongue before taking one into her mouth and sucking hard, causing a ripple of pleasure to go down Samantha's spine.

"Let me have some fun too," Chloe chimed in, her green eyes sparkling with excitement. She circled around the bed, positioning herself behind Samantha as Melissa pushed Samantha on her side. Spreading the girl's ass cheeks, Chloe pressed the tip of her cock against Samantha's tight forbidden hole.

"Fuck, yes," Samantha managed to mumble around Ava's dick as Chloe pushed inside, her cock stretching Samantha's ass to its limits. Samantha squealed at the sensation, her body trembling as all three futas fucked her brutally in unison.

Samantha's world was a whirlwind of pleasure. She could barely keep up with the relentless assault on her senses as the futas worked in perfect harmony to satisfy their mutual desire. Every touch, every kiss, every thrust sent shivers of excitement through her body. The air hummed with their collective moans and gasps, filling the room with an intoxicating symphony of lust.

Victoria positioned herself between Samantha's legs, observing her from above as she leaned in to whisper filthy words into Samantha's ear. "Remember that first night? When you made me feel so alive?" Her breath tickled Samantha's neck, sending chills down her spine. "Now it's our turn."

Emily kneeled beside the bed, stroking herself as she watched Samantha get stretched by Chloe's cock in her ass while Melissa pounded relentlessly inside her pussy. Jasmine alternated between licking Samantha's neck and flicking her nipples, sending electric shockwaves down her core.

As the relentless pounding continued, Samantha caught a glimpse of the remaining futas pairing up and fucking each other passionately. Victoria's hazel eyes met Samantha's as she pumped into Sophia with a snobby grin, while Emily and Jasmine moaned in ecstasy as they pleasured one another. Zoe, ever the mischievous one, eagerly took turns between Emily and Jasmine, ensuring both received equal attention.

"Don't worry, Sam," Ava growled, noticing Samantha's wandering gaze. "They are just warming up for you."

Her body shook with each thrust that pushed her boundaries further and further. She clenched around Melissa's invading cock, squeezing it tightly as she felt Chloe's pistoning behind her.

Victoria's moans echoed in the small space, matching the feral noises coming from Jasmine and Zoe. Chloe's fingers dug into Samantha's hips, leaving bruises that only made her want more.

"Oh fuck..." Samantha groaned around Ava's cock as Melissa picked up the pace, slamming into her deeper and harder than before. She couldn't believe this was happening, yet it felt so right somehow. The sensation of being taken by all these powerful futas was beyond anything she could have imagined. Chloe slowly increased the pace, slamming into Samantha's ass in perfect rhythm with Melissa's thrusts inside her pussy.

She looked up at Ava above her, whose gaze bore into hers with an intensity that promised release. "Don't look away," Ava commanded softly, a hint of domination in her tone. Samantha couldn't tear her eyes away from Ava's stare even if she wanted to—the power emanating from the futa drew her in like a moth to a flame.

"Enough, Melissa," Victoria said, her voice firm as she pushed Melissa off of Samantha. "You've had your share. Now it's my turn."

Without hesitation, Victoria positioned herself between Samantha's legs and slammed her erect cock into her eager pussy. Samantha gasped at the sudden intrusion, a moan escaping her lips as Victoria began pounding her without mercy. With each thrust, the sofa beneath them creaked in protest, but neither woman cared.

"Fuck yeah, take it, you little slut," Victoria growled, her hands gripping Samantha's hips with bruising force. "You wanted this, didn't you? You wanted all of us to fuck you senseless."

Melissa positioned herself on top of Samantha as she jerked off like a feral animal and her cock erupted with a torrent of cum, splashing against Samantha's heaving breasts and reddened cheeks.

"You're even more stunning covered in cum," Melissa praised, her hand tracing across Samantha's sweat-slicked skin as she admired their decadent work of art.

Without warning, a tsunami of pleasure crashed over her as Chloe and Ava came together inside her. Her body shook violently as both futas unloaded copious amounts of cum inside her, filling her mouth and ass until it overflowed.

"Your mouth looks lonely," Emily observed, smirking as she approached Samantha's head. Without waiting for permission, she slid her cock past Samantha's swollen lips, filling her mouth once more, gliding in and out.

On the couch, Melissa, Ava, and Chloe discovered the discarded bag of popcorn, and with wicked grins, they settled in to watch the orgy unfold while snacking on the buttery treat.

"Come on, Sophia! Show her what you got!" Chloe shouted around a mouthful of popcorn.

"Way ahead of you," Sophia replied, guiding Samantha's slick hand to her throbbing cock. "You're going to make me cum, aren't you? Jerk me off like the dirty little slut you are."

Samantha moaned around Emily's cock, her fingers working expertly over Sophia's length, coaxing her towards climax. She could barely keep up with the sensations overwhelming her, from the taste of cum to the pounding between her legs and in her mouth and her empty, but aching ass hole.

Ava watched all four of them, a satisfied smile playing on her lips as she licked popcorn from her fingers.

Victoria, unable to hold back any longer, let out a guttural moan as she reached her climax, filling Samantha's pussy with her hot futa seed. Exhausted but satisfied, Victoria pulled out and stumbled over to the couch, collapsing onto it next to Melissa, Ava, and Chloe.

"Emily, your turn," Victoria panted, wiping sweat from her brow.

Emily grinned and gave one final thrust before pulling her cock out of Samantha's mouth, her own orgasm hitting her like a tidal wave. She sprayed her cum across Samantha's stomach, painting her in thick white streaks.

Samantha's body was a canvas for their pleasure, splattered with the evidence of their uncontained lust.

Zoe, having finished with Jasmine, made her way over to Samantha, her cock glistening under the room's dim light. She grinned down at Samantha, a wicked gleam in her eyes.

"Is our precious little slut ready for another round?" she teased, her fingers trailing up Samantha's thigh.

Samantha could only groan in response—it was all too much. She was spent, yet every touch sent electric sparks shooting through her veins, and she craved more. Victoria threw an arm around Melissa as the chorus of their satisfied laughter filled the room again.

"Finally," Jasmine murmured, her voice husky with lust as she moved into position between Samantha's legs. "I've been waiting for this." Zoe eagerly took Emily's place at Samantha's head, sliding her eager cock into Samantha's waiting mouth.

As Samantha continued jerking Sophia off, she felt the fresh onslaught of pleasure as Jasmine and Zoe began fucking her in unison. Each thrust and moan brought her closer and closer to breaking point, her body quivering with anticipation.

The room was a cacophony of feral moans, sharp breaths, and the slapping of flesh against flesh. Everywhere Samantha looked, she saw hot bodies moving in unison, driven by primal lust. She could feel their sweat dripping onto her from above and below, mixing with the saliva and cum that lubricated the space between them. The scent of sex filled her nostrils, mingling with the buttery popcorn, making for an intoxicating aphrodisiac.

Victoria leaned back against the couch, watching Samantha's efforts to please Sophia while Ava and Chloe fondled each other's breasts. Zoe's cock fucked Samantha's face with relentless force, leaving her gasping for air as she struggled to take it all in. Jasmine grunted above her, their hips slapping together in perfect rhythm with Zoe's thrusts.

"That's it, slut," Zoe growled in approval. "Take it all."

"Come on, Samantha... make me cum!" Sophia urged, her voice strained with the effort of holding back her orgasm.

With a final flick of her wrist, Samantha sent Sophia over the edge. A torrent of hot futa sperm erupted from Sophia's cock, splattering across Samantha's face and coating her in a layer of sticky warmth.

Sophia joined other futas on the couch as Zoe and Jasmine worked Samantha to climax after climax. The room was a blur of pleasure and ecstasy as she became the center of their frenzied love-making, each futa taking her turn to ravish her in different, intoxicating ways.

The scent of sex and popcorn filled the air as the women moved in a synchronized dance of desire and satisfaction. There was no shame, no hesitation—just the pure, primal need to explore each other's bodies.

Jasmine and Zoe continued to thrust into Samantha, driving her past the point of coherent thought. Wave after wave of pleasure washed over her, leaving her breathless and dazed. Every nerve ending sparked with intensity as both women pushed her closer and closer to yet another earth-shattering climax.

Zoe pulled out of Samantha's mouth with a wet pop, leaving her panting for air. "Come on, Jasmine," she said breathlessly, her cock glistening with a mix of saliva and sperm. "Let's make our little slut cum."

Jasmine nodded, her eyes burning with raw desire as she slammed harder into Samantha. The sensation was overwhelming, the heat building in Samantha's lower stomach threatening to explode.

Suddenly, without warning, Jasmine reached down and rubbed her thumb over Samantha's clit, sending her spiraling over the edge. A guttural moan echoed through the room as Samantha came hard around Jasmine's cock, her body shaking with pure ecstasy as waves of pleasure washed over her.

Samantha collapsed onto the soggy carpet, gasping for air as Zoe and Jasmine filled her with their cum.

Samantha came with a force of thousand suns, her body quaking and arching, only to collapse again under the weight of her own pleasure.

Jasmine and Zoe joined the satisfied futas on the couch, panting heavily as they watched Samantha lay spent on the carpet, a vision of absolute decadence and abandon. Her skin glistened with sweat, cum, and saliva— a living tribute to their wild night of pleasure.

As the room fell quiet, save for the panting breaths of those involved, something incredible happened inside Samantha's body. Every square inch of her body, every orifice was filled and covered in futa cum. A single cell of futa sperm found its way into her bloodstream, merging with one of her blood cells. The futa genes within the sperm began splicing into Samantha's DNA, rewriting her very essence.

Slowly, Samantha opened her eyes, and as she looked down at her cum-drenched body, she saw it – a huge cock growing out from between her legs. A smile spread across her face, a mixture of disbelief and excitement. Her days as a futa hunter were over; she was now one of them. And for the first time in her life, she felt like she truly belonged.

The End.

Also by Amanda Strom

Bratty Futas Collection
Bratty Futa Stripper
Bratty Futa Ranger
Bratty Futa Priest

Futa Hunter Collection
Futa Hunter: Sultry Escort
Futa Hunter: Snobby Supermodel
Futa Hunter: Yoga Teacher
Futa Hunter: Awakened

Futa on Futa Fertile Madness Collection
Futa on Futa Means Double Seduction
Futa on Futa Means Double Coffee with Cream
Futa on Futa Means Double Pregnancy: Two Young Women Explore Their Fertility
Futa on Futa Means Double Date
Futa on Futa Means Double Fun
Futa on Futa Means Double Fertility
Futa on Futa Means Double Ecstasy

Futa on Futa Means Double Creaming
Futa on Futa Means Double Pleasure

Futa Travels Collection
Futa Travels: Paris
Futa Travels: Marrakesh
Futa Travels: Rio
Futa Travels: Hollywood
Futa Travels: New Orleans
Futa Travels: Rome
Futa Travels: Bali
Futa Travels: Santorini
Futa Travels: Tokyo

Futa Vixens Collection
Futa Housewife: Neighbor with a Bulge
Futa Plumber
Futa Cop
Futa Maid
Futa Driller
Futa Boss
Futa Fighter
Futa Guard
Futa Coach

Standalone
Futa on Futa Means Double Pleasure Collection: A Bundle of Short
Stories About Fertile Vixens with Bulging Secrets

9 798822 799342